THE HEART OF
MOONLIGHT FALLS

MOONLIGHT FALLS BOOK THREE

COLETTE RIVERA

In the end,
the heart is all that matters.

Content & Trigger Warnings: Anxiety. Social anxiety (character experiencing social anxiety triggers on-page). Past abandonment by a parent and on-page confrontation with that parent. Discussion of taking care of a dying relative in the past. Mention of a past fatal car accident. Death of loved ones (past, off-page) and associated grief. Recollection of a past moment of suicidal ideation. Magical violence. Blood-magic rituals. Fire. On-page possessed animals killed with magic and firearms. On-page undead animals destroyed with magic. Possessed person and on-page exorcism. Self-mutilation: on-page partial finger amputation not done in a medical setting (relating to magic rituals). Grave digging: on-page improper exhumation of bodies. Discussion of self-sacrifice for ritual magic purposes. Sexual content: intended for mature audiences.

Edited by Abbie Nicole

Cover design by Sleepy Fox Studio

End of book illustration by Ladyspiceloaf

People depicted in the cover image and internal images are models and should not be associated with the book.

Interior Formatting by Colette Rivera. Stock Images: Canva Pro

ISBN

Print: 978-1-991284-03-7

Kindle: 978-1-991284-04-4

AUTHOR'S NOTE

Dear reader, if you wish to view content guidance for this book, a list of possible triggers can be found on the copyright page. This book is intended for mature audiences. *The Heart of Moonlight Falls* is the third book in a trilogy that must be read in order. If you haven't started the trilogy, please begin with book one, *The Seduction of James Gray*.

Happy reading!

Storm Family Tree

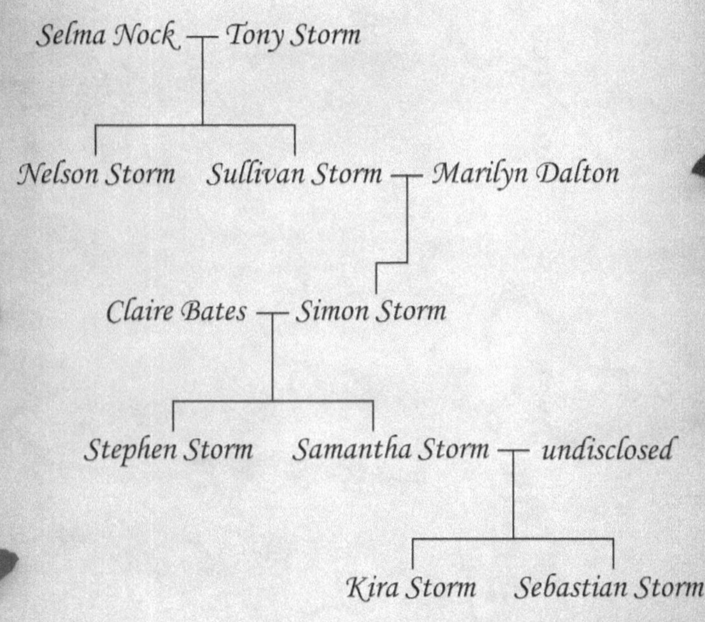

Moonlight Falls Directory

Aydin	Diner Kitchen Hand
Beth	Souvenir Shop Owner
Carla	General Store Clerk
Carson Lee	Logging Foreman
Eleanor Ashley	Mayor
Elijah Gray	Researcher & Diner Waiter
Hazel Delgado	Gray Electrical Co-Owner
James Gray	Gray Electrical Owner
Jay	Town Hall Administrator
Kaylin	Diner Waitress
Luna	Diner Waitress
Melinda Gibbs	City Councilor
Mila Lopez	Librarian
Nora	City Councilor
Parker Hayes	Diner Chef
Princeton Taylor	Museum Curator
Sam Lee	Logger
Sebastian Storm	Owner of Storm Manor
Tony Harris	Elementary School Principal
William	City Councilor

MOONLIGHT FALLS

The Fall of Elijah Gray

The Seduction of James Gray
The Cursed Sebastian Storm
The Heart of Moonlight Falls

THE HEART OF MOONLIGHT FALLS

MOONLIGHT FALLS BOOK THREE

COLETTE RIVERA

JAMES

JAMES HAD ALMOST LOST EVERYTHING. His life, though he hadn't been conscious to realize it, and the man who owned his heart. But he hadn't lost either. Sebastian was right here, in James's bed, alive and even more amazing than James had always thought he was.

He had so many questions but held them back and let Sebastian sleep. James didn't want to bombard him. While Sebastian seemed recovered, James was worried.

No surprise there.

James stroked Sebastian's hair and Sebastian nuzzled into it. He'd never been more anxious than the four days Sebastian had lain in bed, showing no signs of waking.

Sebastian had saved James against impossible odds and pulled him back from a doomed fate. James was in awe and so proud of Sebastian but also infuriated that Sebastian's bravery had put him at such great risk.

James knew his irritation was born out of fear that Sebastian could have died, so he tried to let it go. If James hadn't drained himself so foolishly trying to destroy that shade with fire, he might not have been captured, and Sebastian wouldn't have had to save him. He'd been so worried about keeping everyone else safe that he'd put himself in danger. It was a miracle he and Sebastian both survived.

"I'm sorry," he whispered against Sebastian's hair.

Sebastian stirred. "Why?"

"For making you think you'd lost me."

Sebastian opened his eyes, ginger lashes fluttering. The brown and green flecks in his hazel irises caught the sunlight. "I got you back though. Didn't I? By not waking up and making you worry?" Sebastian's lips twitched.

James shook his head. "This isn't a joke." He smiled anyway. Sebastian's grin was contagious.

Sebastian traced James's curved lips. "Maybe not, but I don't want you brooding over it." He probably didn't want to dwell on how horrible the whole ordeal was either, and James understood that.

"Come on, let's shower and tell the others you've rejoined the land of the living."

A short time later, they entered the kitchen, clean and dressed. James sat Sebastian on a stool at the counter with a glass of water and took out one of the many trays of food Parker had stashed in his fridge.

"Lasagna sound good?"

Sebastian nodded.

"Perfect. It's my favorite." James heated up two plates full of Parker's ricotta and spinach lasagna.

Sebastian seemed ravenous, so James fixed him a second helping. He texted Eli and got an almost instant response, in all caps, saying how relieved Eli was and that he was coming home right away.

"Everyone's coming over, aren't they?" Sebastian asked around a mouthful of food.

James grabbed Sebastian's cup to refill it. "Think so."

Sebastian seemed to brace himself.

"Do you not want them to?"

"No, I do." Sebastian took the water James handed him. "It's just… I know the darkness is gone, but this isn't over." He looked out the kitchen window into the backyard, deep in thought.

Well, that was foreboding.

"Wait…" Sebastian stood abruptly from his stool like all his problems were forgotten. "Are those my chickens?" He turned to James, smiling, adorable dimples framing his face.

"Parker and Eli brought them over. Figured it would be easier to feed them this way."

Sebastian laughed. "Wish I'd been awake to see that."

"I'm sure it was hilarious." James could imagine his brother chasing down the chickens at Storm House. He'd been too distracted at the time to ask if they'd had much trouble.

"James? Sebastian?" Eli's voice called from the front of the house.

"Yeah, we're in here," James called back. He took Sebastian's hand. "If you're still tired, I can talk to them and you can go back upstairs."

"No. It's fine, James."

They headed down the hall to the living room, where Eli, Parker, and Hazel were waiting.

Eli enveloped Sebastian in a hug as quick as humanly possible. "We were so worried."

Sebastian pulled back, blinking wordlessly, and received a shoulder pat from Parker.

Hazel looked Sebastian over like she didn't quite believe he was all right. "Damn near gave me a heart attack when you ran into that horde of shades."

Sebastian grimaced, looking around at them all. "Sorry." He focused on Eli. "You were right about my connection to the veins."

Eli had been almost as stressed as James over the last four days. His hair was a mess and James swore he had worry lines on his face he'd never seen before. "Seems like I was also right about the connection being dangerous to use. If it had killed you, it'd have been all my fault."

"No, it wouldn't have." Sebastian crossed his arms. "If you hadn't told me what you'd suspected about the veins, then I wouldn't have been able to save James, and Moonlight Falls would still be in darkness."

Eli didn't seem reassured, but before he could argue, Parker cut in, "So you *did* banish the darkness? How?"

"We wondered if destroying that giant shade was what brought back the sun," Hazel explained, glancing from Sebastian to James as if looking for answers. James was dying to know the details as much as the rest.

"It wasn't that." Sebastian flopped down in an armchair. "I don't know how I did it exactly." He closed his eyes. "Eli was right. The veins and I are like a unit. I could feel the darkness clinging to us and focused all my energy on it until it burned away. I wasn't really using the veins' power to cast spells. I was harnessing their energy and sending it where I wanted it."

"No wonder it took such a toll on you." James perched on the arm of Sebastian's chair. He wanted to wrap Sebastian up as if holding him tight could protect him from the past.

Sebastian looked at him, eyes tired. "It hurt like hell. But at the time, I thought it wouldn't work, and while it's great things turned out okay, I'm really hoping I don't have to do it again."

"Why would you have to do it again?" James laid a hand on Sebastian's shoulder. "The shade is gone. If it's so hard for complex beings to come into our world, I doubt it will return to Moonlight Falls."

"Yeah, that attack seems like a once-in-a-lifetime event," Hazel agreed from the couch opposite them.

Sebastian tensed beneath James's hand. "Have there been many shades around?"

"We've hardly seen any," Parker assured him, and Eli nodded in agreement.

Sebastian didn't relax. "Even at Storm House?"

Eli perched on the couch next to Hazel. "We haven't been out there at night." He looked quickly at Parker, hovering beside him, then away.

Sebastian shifted in his seat, avoiding everyone's eye. "So they could be regrouping and we wouldn't know."

James squeezed his shoulder. "Regrouping? What do you mean?"

Sebastian's gaze found James, his expression even more exhausted than before. "I think I know where all the shades are coming from. And I think I know why the energy pattern at the intersection looks so weird."

Eli's posture stiffened. "Really?"

Sebastian kept his focus on James. "I think the vein intersection's energy resembles what we see in shifting veins because, like shifting veins, the intersection is a gateway to Beyond."

Sebastian watched comprehension wash over James's face. His eyes widened, but Sebastian didn't think James doubted his claim.

"Just because the energy looks similar doesn't mean the intersection is creating a passage between our worlds," Eli argued. "They're still fixed veins."

Sebastian tore his gaze from James. "You can test it all you want, but that shade-thing called me a gatekeeper. It seemed to know I couldn't leave Moonlight Falls. Like maybe it knew I was tied to the veins. I think it has a much better understanding of what was happening than we do. It makes sense for the intersection to be a gateway when there have always been so many more shades on my property than anywhere else."

"It explains why so many shades are in and around Moonlight Falls," Hazel added, though she didn't look pleased by the idea. "We've always wondered why they come here specifically."

"I'd love to know how many shades there were in the area before my ancestors messed with the veins." Sebastian rubbed his brow, a headache building behind his eyes. "I bet there weren't many." If Sebastian was a gatekeeper, his uncle and everyone who came before him must have been one too. "Storms have been holding the veins stable and apparently holding a passage to Beyond open. So until we figure out how to solve the imbalance and return the veins to their natural, stable state, the passage will stay open and that shade could return. It said as much to me before I banished it."

I will come back. Beyond isn't for the living.

The words echoed in Sebastian's head, the memory of the shade's eerie voice giving him chills.

There was a heavy silence in the living room.

"Well, if we weren't motivated to solve the imbalance before, we are now," Hazel said dryly.

Eli and Parker shared a quick look of alarm, but Eli's focus immediately returned to Sebastian. "The humanoid shade can't have come back yet. If it had, surely it wouldn't wait to attack again."

"Maybe." Sebastian shrugged. That didn't mean it wasn't still coming. Maybe the shade needed to bide its time and get its strength back. Either way, it wasn't gone for good.

James studied Sebastian, worry lining his face. "If it does come back, you can't fight it off again."

Sebastian didn't want to disagree, and even more than that, he didn't want to worry James. "But I don't see any other way to beat it. It was way too powerful."

"Then we'll need to get actual assistance next time. If there is a next time." James scowled, clearly determined to protect Sebastian from this. "Eleanor was right. Attacks from Beyond are not our responsibility to fight off."

"Getting help if this happens again might not be so easy," Hazel grumbled, slouching against the couch. "By the time anyone from out of town got here, things were back to normal and the officials started questioning Eleanor like they didn't believe there'd ever been an invasion."

James's brows flew up in shock. "You're kidding?"

Sebastian's heart sank.

"No." Hazel bit her lip in apparent frustration. "It's classic misogyny, really. Acting like Eleanor overreacted to the darkness and doesn't know what she's talking about rather than believing what she says. Like they can't trust her first-hand account."

"Why didn't you tell me Eleanor was having so much trouble?" James asked.

Hazel looked at him helplessly. "You had more than enough to worry about, James. And it's not like there's anything you could have done about the state not believing a shadow-being from Beyond tried to overtake the town. Of course, Eleanor has no idea how the invasion was stopped, which didn't help when she was trying to explain. But even now that we know what Sebastian did, it's not like we can tell her."

Hazel's voice rose along with the tension in the room. Sebastian's headache intensified, the familiar guilty feeling growing inside him doing nothing to help. They couldn't explain to Eleanor how he'd defeated the shade or banished the darkness without telling her about the veins and the curse.

"She knows we're hiding something," Hazel added. "She hasn't forgotten that I let slip we couldn't leave Moonlight Falls and won't stop asking me what I meant."

"Shit." James rubbed at his stubble-lined face.

"Not that this is the most important aspect of the whole mess, but lying to her is screwing with our relationship." Hazel heaved a heavy sigh. "She keeps accusing me of not trusting her."

"I'm so sorry, Hazel. But the only alternative to keeping it secret is trapping her," James said as if the words pained him. "If a gateway to Beyond is sitting open at Storm House, and there's a good chance that shade-thing will come back and do this all over again, we *can't* get her stuck here with us."

"I know," Hazel growled. "I don't want her trapped here if it's going to get dangerous."

Eli and Parker shared another apprehensive look.

Sebastian pointed at them. "What's with you two?"

Eli's eyes went wide. "Um…"

Parker put a hand on Eli's shoulder. "We might as well lay out all the problems."

Eli slumped, seeming almost guilty. "We've been collecting the data from Storm House and noticed the fuel cell is draining a lot quicker than before. The energy levels in the veins are higher too. And after Sebastian said he burned the darkness away using the veins, I think that could have made things less stable, and that's why we're seeing these changes. It would have been a huge amount of energy passing through a system that was already precarious."

Sebastian put his head in his hands. He couldn't deal with any of this right now, and it wasn't just because his head was killing him.

"How much quicker is the fuel cell draining?" James asked as he rubbed Sebastian's back.

"It's hard to say." Eli didn't sound confident. "It's a bit all over the place."

James's hand paused on Sebastian's back. "Let's go out and take a look."

Sebastian forced himself to sit up.

James caught his eye, a tender smile pulling at his lips. "You can stay here if you want."

It was a tempting offer. Sebastian no longer felt it was solely his responsibility to fix all this or that he had to solve problems to keep people happy with him so he wouldn't be abandoned, but he wouldn't be able to relax and rest if he stayed behind. He might as well go.

Sebastian stood. "I just need some painkillers, and then let's head out."

James caught his arm. "If you aren't feeling well, you should go back to bed."

"I'm not going to be able to sleep. All I'll end up doing is wondering what you all are seeing in the clearing."

James nodded in understanding, concerned gaze raking over Sebastian. "What hurts?"

Sebastian rubbed his brow again, even though doing so wasn't helping. "My head."

James pressed a gentle hand to Sebastian's cheek. "Do you think it's from the magic you did?"

"I don't know, maybe." Sebastian followed James to the downstairs bathroom, where James opened the medicine cabinet. "Using the veins made my head feel like it was splitting open. This feels nowhere near as bad."

James handed over a bottle of painkillers with a strained expression. "Will you let me know if anything else feels off?"

Sebastian swallowed a pill. "Definitely. I really hope there aren't any lasting effects from using the veins." Fear that he'd hurt himself in some irreversible way hit Sebastian for the first time. He hadn't had a chance to worry about it before.

James brushed a stray lock of Sebastian's hair from his brow. "I hope not too, but I'll look after you either way."

"Thank you," Sebastian murmured, his heart aching.

James squeezed his shoulder, affection radiating out of him in everything from his touch to the set of his brow. "I've got you, Sebastian. You're mine, remember?"

"Yeah." Sebastian returned James's soft look. "But I still like hearing that it hasn't changed."

"Your truck is back." Sebastian paused as he and James entered the garage. He hadn't thought he'd be so pleased to see the familiar vehicle.

"Good as new." James patted the hood before climbing in.

"I'm taking it as a sign of good things to come that we're

returning to normal." Sebastian climbed into the passenger seat. "James in his jacket, driving his truck."

James shook his head. "Thought you might want the jacket back."

That was a good point. "True. In that case, things are returning to a better version of normal."

James snorted. "Fuck, I love your optimism. You don't stay down long."

Sebastian's cheeks heated at the admiration in James's tone. "I guess I've had a lot of practice pushing through the worst."

James squeezed his knee. "True, but now you've got me to help you. We'll figure this out. We'll get through it."

"I sure hope so." Sebastian leaned back in his seat. He closed his eyes in an attempt to rest his head as James drove.

Despite everything, it felt good to face things with James and not have any secrets between them. It was ridiculous what a difference trust made, even when his faith in James was the only thing Sebastian was sure of. Everything else was up in the air and likely to be a disaster, but Sebastian knew he wasn't facing it alone.

They would take care of each other.

Storm House seemed the same as ever. Eli had driven the others in his car, and they all trooped up the driveway together. The sun was still shining brightly, so there were no shades. Part of Sebastian wanted to come out at night and camp out in the house just to see how many of the beasts were there, but the other part was still afraid to set foot back inside, especially after dark.

As soon as they reached the clearing, Sebastian noticed something was wrong with the fuel cell. It looked off-kilter, like it was tipping slightly to one side.

James crouched to inspect the base. "It's sinking into the ground."

"I don't remember it being like that yesterday," Eli said from beside James.

Parker put his hand on Eli's shoulder. "Me either."

James stood and looked at the indicator lights. "How's this compared to when you were last here?" He pointed to the lights.

Eli had a look. "It's dropped, but not as badly as when we first came out after the darkness disappeared."

James nodded. "So most of this power was lost fighting the darkness?"

"Maybe half." Eli opened his notebook. "There was another big drop yesterday."

"Okay." James scratched his chin. "Even if it keeps dropping this much every day, we won't need to replace the fuel cell for a month or more. So, no immediate danger."

"Unless it starts dropping faster," Hazel cut in.

"We need to keep a close eye on it for sure," James agreed.

Sebastian stared at the base of the fuel cell sinking into the ground. Was the dirt too soft? He wouldn't have thought so. His head pounded dully and he hoped the painkillers would start working soon.

"Could you tell anything else about the veins, Sebastian?"

Eli's question pulled Sebastian out of his daze. "Like what?"

"Anything that felt wrong or like something that needed to be fixed?" Eli gave him a hopeful look.

"No." Sebastian had no idea how the veins worked, even though they were apparently connected to him. "I don't want to delve back into them to try and check either," he admitted. "I don't actually know if I could get the connection back. It happened mostly by accident."

The moment he'd connected to the veins had been so hopeless. The vision of being dead and buried wasn't one Sebastian wanted to revisit.

"I don't think you should try anything like that," Eli said quickly.

James nodded at his brother. "Me either."

Sebastian was grateful they were all in agreement but didn't know how they were going to solve the problem. They had no new ideas.

"There must be a way to figure out how the veins were broken in the first place so we can work backward and find a solution," Sebastian said, not bothering to disguise the pleading in his voice. He'd searched the house and found nothing that hinted at what exactly had caused the imbalance but maybe they could solve the puzzle another way.

"I'll keep collecting data and doing research." Eli bent to uncover one of the mechanisms. "I haven't found anything helpful about imbalances yet, but I've still got a lot of resources to go through."

Sebastian wasn't sure that was enough. He appreciated Eli and knew he was doing everything he could. He just wished they had more than one avenue to explore.

They collected the receipts and added new rolls of paper to the mechanisms. With nothing else useful to do, they drove back to town.

3

JAMES

ELI DISAPPEARED off to Parker's when they returned from Storm House. He'd been staying with James each night while Sebastian lay unconscious, but James insisted Eli didn't need to keep him company again that night.

Sebastian went to sleep as soon as they got back. James let him rest and only hovered a little.

Around dinner time, James climbed into bed with Sebastian, planning to wake him to eat soon. Parker had given them a pot of vegetarian chili, which James thought Sebastian would enjoy, but before James could decide how to wake Sebastian, he opened his eyes.

"Hey, there." He wiggled closer to James, who'd gotten under the covers with him.

"How are you feeling?"

"Much better. My head is clear." Sebastian ran his hand over James's bare chest. "You got undressed."

James wore only his boxer briefs, the same as Sebastian. "I wasn't going to wake you up right away."

"Mm," Sebastian hummed. "What were you going to do?" He bit his bottom lip and raised his eyebrows.

15

James shook his head and attempted to repress a grin. "I was going to hold you. Maybe stroke your hair."

"My sweet James." Sebastian pressed closer. "But now that I'm awake, we can get more creative than that."

"Can we?" James tried to play it coy and failed. Sebastian turned him on so damn much, and coming so close to losing him made James yearn for every bit of closeness they could have.

Sebastian hitched a leg around James. "I'm thinking yes."

James threaded his fingers through Sebastian's curls and took his mouth in a deep kiss that wasn't just about sexual attraction but connection. James needed to release all his feelings. He needed to kiss Sebastian roughly and give him all his affection, knowing it always made Sebastian moan and melt in his arms. "Tell me what you need, sweetheart."

Sebastian whined, his cock hardening against James's stomach. "What about what you need, James?"

"I've got it right here. Need to make you feel good." He kissed down Sebastian's neck, just how he liked.

"You always do." Sebastian arched into him. "But we always do what I want. What about you?"

James paused. He wanted to please Sebastian, to show him he was chosen and cherished. But James knew what Sebastian meant. He almost always deferred to Sebastian when choosing *how* they came together.

"How can I take care of you tonight?" Sebastian slipped his hand into James's boxer briefs and cupped his balls, then slid his hand up to grip James's growing erection.

Their eyes locked, and Sebastian waited, stroking lazily. What did James want, and why did asking for it make him feel so exposed?

James pushed his hesitation away and let his imagination take over. An erotic image filled his mind, and he knew he needed it to become a reality. "Would you fuck me?" he breathed.

Sebastian's grin turned wicked. "I'd love to. I didn't realize you were interested in bottoming."

"I don't do it often." James's cheeks burned. "Besides, I like giving you what you want, and I know you like me fucking you."

Sebastian cocked his head. "Is that why you haven't asked to bottom before?"

James shrugged. It wasn't quite the reason. "I like giving you pleasure. But, um… I have to be in the right mood to want someone fucking me. It has to be with the right person."

Sebastian smiled at that, not a hint of mischievousness in sight. It was all tender affection. "I get that." He pressed his lips close to James's ear. "Fucking you would give me lots of pleasure."

James swallowed. "Yeah. I hope it would."

Sebastian ran a hand down James's body. "And are you in the right mood, babe?"

"Yes, I am," James rasped. His eyes fluttered closed for a second, and he let how much he wanted this consume him.

Sebastian hummed. "I like it when you tell me what you want. When you ask for things."

Of course Sebastian would like that. James was practically addicted to the reverse. And lying here, pressed together, the way Sebastian looked at him, James liked this just as much. He could do with more of it in his life.

James had slowly opened up and was ready to throw the doors wide open. He didn't have to worry about rejection or judgment with Sebastian. He could let go of all the reserved pieces of his personality he'd used to protect his heart and express any desire he had.

"I liked it when you played with my hole," James confessed.

"Mm. I could tell." Sebastian tugged James's underwear off, then removed his own. "Want me to do it again?"

"Yes." James shivered.

Sebastian grabbed lube out of the bedside table drawer. Back on the bed, he threw the blankets aside and looked down at James splayed beneath him. James bent his legs and spread them wide.

Sebastian's attention fixed on James's core as he opened the lube. "Seeing you like this gives me all kinds of ideas."

James let out an involuntary whine of anticipation. "I'm sure it does."

Sebastian's fingers delved between his legs, seeking out his hole. James bit his lip and moaned softly at the contact. Sebastian rubbed his rim with slick fingers until he relaxed more fully, then pressed his finger in.

"Oh fuck." James squirmed.

"You're so tight, babe." Sebastian rubbed James's taint with his other hand as he worked his finger inside. "Is that good squirming, or is it uncomfortable?"

"No, it's good. Just…" James took a breath. "Keep going."

Sebastian pumped his finger in and out. "Tell me when you're ready for more."

James nodded. He was hot, sweat prickling along his forehead. It had been a while since he'd had anything inside him, but it didn't take long to get used to the sensation. The more Sebastian touched him, the more he wanted.

The second finger stung when Sebastian breached him, but James wanted to be stretched and the discomfort didn't last long. He was caught up in how gorgeous Sebastian looked, looming above him. His soft skin glowed in the evening light, freckles dusting his shoulders and cheeks, his tousled, curly hair in his eyes. Every time Sebastian peeked at James's face, James's heart stuttered.

James whimpered and groaned—he was desperate—and they'd barely started. He wasn't sure he'd ever made this much noise during sex. When Sebastian found his prostate, he lost it completely. He moaned and swore, his cock leaking onto his stomach.

"Fuck me, Sebastian." James thrust against Sebastian's fingers.

He had to be up to three by now, but he was so far gone it was hard to be sure.

Sebastian withdrew. "Let me get a condom."

"Wait." James grabbed Sebastian's hand. He felt empty, and his mind spun. He needed Sebastian. "We don't have to use one."

Sebastian paused. "True, we're both negative. I thought, since you always use one..?"

"It was just habit. I've never not used a condom." James's heart pounded. He wanted Sebastian back inside him. To feel that special closeness.

"I haven't either." Sebastian's cheeks flushed dark red. "Fuck, I really want this, James. With you."

"Me too."

Sebastian slathered his bare cock with lube. James hitched his knees up and Sebastian lined himself up, rubbing his cockhead over James's hole.

"Please," James begged.

He always loved hearing Sebastian's pleas, and it seemed Sebastian felt the same about his. He groaned and thrust forward, stretching James, pushing in with nothing between them.

"Oh fuck," Sebastian whined as he bore down. "You feel so good, babe."

James let his legs fall and wrapped them around Sebastian. His breaths came out in hard pants. He'd enjoyed bottoming in the past, but there was a reason it wasn't his preference. He found it hard to get out of his head when someone was filling him and had always assumed there'd be as much discomfort as pleasure. It wasn't like that this time. He trusted Sebastian enough to not need to think. He wasn't worried or self-conscious. He was free to fall into the good sensations, making the overwhelming fullness not only enjoyable when it was Sebastian stretching him but something he couldn't get enough of.

His hands found their way to Sebastian's shoulders and pulled him close. Sebastian thrust forward until his hips met James's ass, and James wrapped his arms around Sebastian's neck.

James couldn't have formed a coherent thought if he'd tried. He was stuffed tight. Sebastian was everything, and it all felt so good.

They kissed and panted into each other's mouths. Sebastian thrust slowly at first, but when James started meeting his thrusts with firm ones of his own, Sebastian snapped his hips, sending a jolt through James's whole body.

"Sebastian," he groaned. "Don't stop."

Sebastian didn't. He took James apart like no one else ever had. James couldn't think beyond the feeling of Sebastian inside him, and he loved it. He just existed in this special space where there was nothing but the man who was everything to him.

"Fuck yeah, James." Sebastian's chest glowed with a sheen of sweat. He pumped his hips, looking down to see their bodies joining. "You're perfect."

James felt like it. This moment was perfect. He wanted to convey that but found himself begging instead. "Please, Sebastian. I need…please." He didn't know what he was asking. He was getting everything he wanted.

Sebastian seemed to be in control of his brain and responded as if he knew what James was babbling about. "I've got you. You need more?"

James nodded, and Sebastian sat back, grabbed James's legs, and ran his hands along his thighs to his calves before gripping his ankles and bringing James's feet over his shoulders.

James's body tilted. "Sebastian." He arched as Sebastian's dick thrust deeper, swiping over that sweet spot inside him, and moaned for all he was worth.

Sebastian was absolutely beautiful as he fucked James, head thrown back, exposing his pale neck and the fading bite-mark bruises on his shoulder. "Oh, James. James," he chanted, hips snapping.

It was so intense. James needed release. He had to come before his brain exploded, overwhelmed with too many erotic images and feelings. He took hold of his aching dick and stroked. Sebastian hit his prostate again, and James came on a shout.

Sebastian gazed down at him with heavy-lidded eyes. His thrusts turned erratic, then he stiffened and flooded James with his cum.

James whimpered as Sebastian filled him. Sebastian held his stare, and James had never felt closer to another person. He was wrecked, exposed, and aching with affection for the man he'd let take him apart.

Eventually, Sebastian pulled out and lowered James's legs so he could lie on top of him. James wrapped his arms around Sebastian but couldn't manage to move more than that.

"Oh my god, James. That was amazing." Sebastian nuzzled the side of his jaw.

James's hole ached. "No one's ever fucked me that well."

Sebastian preened, his dimples making an appearance. "No one's ever filled you up either."

James would have blushed if he wasn't already hot all over. "No, that's just for you."

Sebastian nipped his ear. "Mine."

James tightened his arms around him. "Yours."

THE NEXT MORNING WAS MONDAY, but James didn't get up and go to work. He figured he'd go in that afternoon if everything was fine with Sebastian. After the epic pounding Sebastian had given James the night before, James didn't doubt he was well recovered, but the headache he'd had yesterday was worrying.

James's body ached as he got up. He winced at how tender his hole was, not that he wished Sebastian had gone easier on him. He wanted to do it all over again.

He let images from last night play over in his mind as he dressed. Eventually, he made himself think of other things, or he wouldn't have been able to resist waking Sebastian and losing himself in him again.

Downstairs, James's phone rang as the coffee brewed. He answered it.

"Hello, James?" Eleanor's voice came through the speaker.

"Yeah, hi. How are you doing?"

Eleanor made a frustrated sound. "Never mind that. I heard Sebastian is doing better."

James confirmed.

"Would you mind asking him if he can stop by my office? I'd like to know what happened with that shade."

"I'll talk to him when he wakes up." James couldn't fight off the sinking feeling in his gut. He didn't know what to do about Eleanor.

After the mayor hung up, James called Hazel. She didn't think it was a good idea to avoid Eleanor. Sebastian could say he wasn't up for explaining today, but they couldn't put it off indefinitely. Hazel said she'd meet James at town hall and see Eleanor with him and Sebastian. James was relieved because anything they told the mayor would seem like something Hazel was hiding from her, and James didn't want to cause more problems than the two women already had.

James cooked eggs and pancakes for Sebastian, who seemed to come downstairs just in time for the food to be ready. James filled him in as they ate.

"I can try to bullshit my way through." Sebastian piled his plate with a second helping of pancakes. "Pretend I did some sort of lightning spell, maybe? But if anyone asks me to do it again, it's not happening."

"That might be the best we can do," James agreed. He didn't want to lie to Eleanor, but what choice did they have?

4

SEBASTIAN

S EBASTIAN AND J AMES found Hazel waiting for them on the sidewalk in front of town hall. The front entrance was blocked off since the reception area had been destroyed in the fire, and a team of workers were replacing the busted glass above the doorway. Sebastian carefully stepped around the mess of cones and ladders, following James and Hazel to the back entrance.

Inside, Eleanor's office door was open. As they entered, the mayor seemed surprised to see Hazel but didn't comment.

She folded her hands in front of her on the desk. "How are you, Sebastian?"

"Much better, thank you." He shifted uncomfortably as he took a seat.

"We were all very worried. I'm surprised you didn't go to the hospital."

Sebastian didn't know how to respond. If he'd wanted to, he could have said he was unable to go to the hospital, meaning the secret-binding was as weak as ever. He almost wished it hadn't worn so thin. The secret-binding would have helped him lie more convincingly, but as it was, it felt like nothing held him back from spilling Storm House's secrets.

Eleanor eyed him closely as he failed to speak. She looked tired, and Sebastian felt bad for contributing to her stress. At last, Eleanor moved on. "How did you manage to destroy that shade-being?"

"A lightning spell with a lot of energy. I had to think of something since the fire didn't work. It was a long shot, but, well..." His words faded.

Eleanor blinked, taking a beat to absorb Sebastian's statement. "You have that much power?" she asked, her tone implying she didn't believe him. Maybe she was wondering why he hadn't done the lightning spell sooner. When Sebastian didn't respond beyond a quick nod, she went on. "And the darkness?"

Sebastian forced himself to maintain eye contact. "I'm not really sure. It disappeared with the shade."

Eleanor paused like she was waiting for more. Eventually, she asked, "And why didn't you leave Moonlight Falls?"

"I didn't have to in the end. Things were so hectic, then it was all over."

Eleanor looked far from convinced. She turned to James and Hazel. "And you two? Why couldn't you leave? Why not take Sebastian to the hospital when he didn't wake up?" When no one answered right away, Eleanor stood. She leaned forward, bracing her palms on the desk. "What are you hiding? I don't get it. I thought we were a team. I don't see why you're trying to make it harder for me to deal with this than it already is. I know you all have Moonlight Falls' best interest at heart."

"Eleanor, please," Hazel begged, hands fisting the ends of her shirt sleeves. "This is for your own good."

"*My what?*" Eleanor straightened, crossing her arms. "How? Keeping secrets isn't protecting or helping me. It's doing the opposite. I need to know what happened. Otherwise, the officials will never believe me. What if this happens again, and next time, they don't send help?"

Hazel stood, facing Eleanor. "It potentially happening again is exactly why we can't tell you anything."

The mayor narrowed her eyes, saying slowly, "Because you couldn't leave." She pursed her lips like she was putting all the small pieces she'd picked up together. "You *really* couldn't leave, and if it happens again, what? I suddenly won't want to leave if I know what you're hiding?"

Hazel turned helplessly to James and Sebastian.

"You know I'm dedicated to this town," Eleanor went on. "I'll do whatever it takes. All I'm asking for is your cooperation and for you to trust me."

This situation wasn't helping anyone. They couldn't trap Eleanor against her will, but what if she knew the stakes? What if she accepted the risk freely?

Sebastian leaned forward in his chair. "Whatever it takes? Are you sure?"

"Yes," Eleanor said adamantly.

Hazel sucked in a breath. "Sebastian."

"It can be her choice." He held Hazel's stare, and she nodded in agreement. When Sebastian's gaze landed on James, he nodded as well.

Sebastian turned back to Eleanor. Her expression was tight. Sebastian hoped she would decline his offer, even if he was willing to let her decide. "What if I told you explaining had a price? We aren't acting like this because we want to." The words came out easily. Sebastian wondered if Eleanor would even have to break what was left of the secret-binding. If she didn't, was there a chance she wouldn't be trapped? That felt like too much to hope for.

Eleanor returned to her chair. "What price? What do you mean?"

Sebastian braced himself. "We can't physically leave Moonlight Falls. Learning what we know will magically trap you too."

Eleanor's eyes went wide. "Meaning, if there's another attack,

I won't be able to evacuate." She glanced at Hazel, who nodded. "Tell me," Eleanor said without hesitation.

"Are you sure?" Hazel pressed.

"If you're trapped here, really trapped, you know I'm not leaving you behind, Hazel. Free or not." Eleanor's gaze turned warm as she studied the other woman.

Hazel ran a hand over her face. "You're right. There's no way I'd get you to leave me behind. I just wanted to save you from this."

"I understand," Eleanor said softly. "But we're in this together."

They didn't need to break the secret-binding and the longer Sebastian explained—he started at the beginning—the easier the words came.

He wondered if whatever had happened to the veins when he'd banished the darkness had further weakened the secret-binding spell. Was whatever aspect of the curse Selma had linked the secret-binding to responding to the changing veins, or had the increased instability in the veins broken the link the secret-binding had to the rest of the curse?

By the time Sebastian was done talking, Eleanor had her hands fisted in her short hair, elbows braced on her desk. "So the whole area might blow up. We have a portal for shades and even worse beasts from Beyond sitting on your property. And all four of us are trapped here?"

"Eli and Parker are trapped too," James corrected.

Eleanor let go of her hair and stared at them. "What a clusterfuck."

"Sorry." Sebastian couldn't help apologizing. The shade problems and invasion from Beyond might not have been directly caused by his family, but they'd been the ones to let the beasts in.

"No need to apologize." Eleanor made a visible effort to collect herself, smoothing her hair. "This is the kind of thing I need to be aware of. I'm glad you told me. I understand magic stopped you asking for help before now, but at least we're past that."

"Maybe you'll be able to relay the whole story to the officials since it was easier for Sebastian to tell you today than it was before." Hazel looked hopeful. "I tried to report it last week but was tongue-tied."

Eleanor picked up her desk phone. Sebastian held his breath as she made the call. At first, it all sounded fine, but when she began her explanation, Eleanor's words seemed to stick in her throat. She passed the phone to Sebastian for him to try. He failed too and passed the phone back.

Giving up, Eleanor slammed the receiver down. "Why can't we tell them as easily as you told me?"

Sebastian chewed his lower lip, thinking. "We've seen the curse respond to changes in the vein system before when the area we were trapped in expanded after adding the fuel cell into the mix. Now, as the veins get less stable, things seem to be falling apart. The energy in the fuel cell is draining erratically and the secret-binding doesn't seem to be working properly but, unfortunately, isn't completely broken."

James turned to Sebastian. "Do you think the secret-binding only prevents us from telling people outside Moonlight Falls?"

"Seems that way," Sebastian agreed. "We still can't get beyond the reach of the veins, even with words. It's like the part of the curse meant to contain everything is still holding on strong."

"So we can only tell people within the veins' area? People we can trap?" Eleanor asked.

"Are you planning to tell anyone other than people outside who might help?" James looked at her in alarm. "We really shouldn't tell and trap anyone else. Just because things are falling apart and telling you was easy doesn't mean the curse hasn't spread to you."

Eleanor sagged in her chair. "I know. And no, of course, I won't be spreading this around. You have my word. I'll double-check if I've been trapped but will assume I have been until then." She drummed her fingers on her desk, thinking for a moment. "If there's a chance the town might explode, I need to act fast. It won't be easy to get everything in motion without the city councilors signing off on certain things, but I'll figure it out and have an evacuation plan and potential shelter options in place as soon as possible."

"If there's anything we can do to help with that, let us know," Sebastian offered.

"Thank you." Eleanor gave him a grim smile.

Sebastian and James left town hall while Hazel stayed behind. Sebastian hoped there'd be less tension between her and Eleanor and was glad there were no more forced secrets between them, but he didn't feel entirely good about spreading his curse.

Outside, James stared across the street at the stone in the center of the road, seeming deep in thought.

"Did I do the right thing?" Sebastian asked, unable to hold the question in even though there was no taking it back now. He longed for a nap, exhausted as if he hadn't just woken up an hour ago.

"Yes, Sebastian. You made it Eleanor's choice." James put a comforting hand on Sebastian's arm. "She'll do whatever she can for the town. More than we could—"

A roar cut across James's words, and he fell silent.

Sebastian stepped closer to him. "What was that?"

Someone screamed.

James's hand on Sebastian tightened. "It sounded like it was coming from over by the diner."

They jogged across the street without hesitation. Another scream and a louder, snarling roar cut across the quiet circle.

"It can't be a shade," Sebastian muttered, hoping he wasn't wrong. The last thing they needed was light-resistant ones out on a sunlit day.

A woman darted into a car parked in front of the park as a

bear paced back and forth beside it. One of the picnic tables behind it was crushed.

Sebastian grabbed James, forcing them both to stop on the edge of the grass surrounding the stone. "What are the chances that's a normal bear?"

The animal turned its head toward them, revealing onyx eyes and a chunk of flesh missing from its face.

James swallowed. "I'd say zero."

Fuck, it was possessed. The longer Sebastian looked, the more wrong the bear seemed. Its fur was matted with dirt, its skin hanging loosely in some areas but not others. There were wounds on its side and chest, but the blood was black and dried.

It roared, flecks of something flying from its mouth. The bear abandoned the car and stalked toward them.

"Fuck, fuck, fuck." Sebastian tried to drag James backward. Why had they come over here? They couldn't save anyone from a possessed predator.

James sent sparks at the bear. The embers landed in the fur on its chest and ignited. The beast jolted and growled but kept moving, burning as it walked toward them like nothing was wrong.

"Why isn't it stopping?" James gasped, bewildered.

"I think it's already dead. Look." Sebastian pointed. "It's half-decayed."

"Is it the same bear Carson's son shot in the woods?"

At this point, it didn't matter. The horror that had once been a bear was coming closer. The fire spread up the beast's shoulders, but the shade inside seemed unbothered, its dark eyes fixed on its prey.

Usually, you had to kill a possessed animal to get the shade to leave the body. Sebastian didn't know what to do if the animal was already dead.

"Aim for its eyes," Sebastian yelled, taking a guess and hoping that hitting the shade's eyes would vanquish the beast.

He and James sent sparks and ran. The bear wouldn't even need to bite them or swipe them with its claws to kill them. It would just knock them down with a flaming paw and set them on fire.

Parker burst out of the diner behind them. "Hey!"

The bear paused at the sound and turned. It hesitated as it tried to decide who to pursue.

One sure way to get rid of the possessed beast occurred to Sebastian. He was on the south side of the circle this time, but the vein was still underfoot.

It didn't take the complete, hopeless desire to die to connect to the vein this time. Sebastian just had to focus under the earth, knowing part of him was down there, and pull.

His fingers crackled blue.

The bear turned back toward him and James and lunged, flaming paws launching into the air as it barred its onyx teeth. Sebastian shot pure, hot power at it, his nerves burning with the effort.

Blue energy cut through the fire and hit the bear in the chest. It screeched, but unlike the roaring from earlier, this was high-pitched. Shadow burst from the burning bear and dissipated as the body crumpled to the ground in a putrid heap.

Sebastian dropped to his knees, panting heavily, his head pounding like his heart and brain had swapped places. He released the power of the veins, but it didn't help. He groaned.

"Sebastian!" James wrapped his arms around him and pulled him against his chest.

A moment later, Parker was on his other side. Sebastian closed his eyes. He swore he could hear the sound of a fire extin-guisher, but less and less was penetrating the pain in his head.

He just needed to sleep. A little nap, that was all.

5

JAMES

JAMES AND PARKER took Sebastian to his duplex. He was alive, his pulse steady, but James wished they could have taken him to a hospital instead.

The sight of Sebastian unconscious in his bed made James sick with worry. His stomach cramped and he couldn't get it to settle. From everything James had heard about Sebastian's fight with the invading shade, he'd used way more power that day, yet he was knocked out from just one blast today.

James sat in bed next to Sebastian. He wasn't shivering like he had been when he'd used too much magic at Storm House, so James hoped that was a good sign. He clung to the fact that Sebastian's condition didn't seem to worsen. There wasn't much more he could do than wait. Even if he found a doctor who made house calls, he couldn't explain what Sebastian had done with the vein's power without revealing the curse.

It was a long afternoon.

Sebastian finally stirred as the sun set. He blinked and looked around in confusion but seemed to become alert much quicker than when he'd woken from his four-day sleep.

"We're at the duplex?" Sebastian sat up and leaned against James, the contact an immense relief.

"Yeah. Do you remember what happened?"

Sebastian rubbed his eyes. "The bear." He turned toward the window and the darkening sky. "How long was I out?"

"Several hours. It's still Monday."

Sebastian nodded. "Oh, good. Not too long." He sounded exhausted.

James stroked Sebastian's hair. "Want to come downstairs and have something to eat? Or I can bring it up for you?" James didn't know what else to do.

"I don't have anything here that you won't have to cook. We could boil some pasta and open a can of something to put on it."

"Parker and Eli are in the living room. They brought food over." James hadn't been able to get rid of them. They were worried about Sebastian, and James suspected they were worried about him too.

Sebastian smiled. "That was nice of them. Let's go down."

James stayed close to Sebastian on the stairs, but he seemed steady enough.

"Good to see you standing, Sebastian," Parker said as they entered the living room. He and Eli were settled on the couch, Parker reading a book while Eli worked.

Eli closed his laptop. "How do you feel?"

"Tired." Sebastian took a seat at the dining table. "But something smells good."

"That'll be Parker's pumpkin soup." James joined Sebastian at the table, not able to leave his side.

"*Ugh*, my pumpkins," Sebastian groaned. "Some of them have got to be past ripe by now. They're going to rot away."

Parker got up and headed to the kitchen. "Eli and I have kept an eye on your veggies. Don't worry."

Sebastian blinked in surprise. "Wow. Thanks."

They ate, and Sebastian seemed just as hungry as he'd been

the day before. He might not be using his magic when he harnessed that blue power, but it sure depleted his energy.

"I thought you weren't going to try to connect to the veins again," James couldn't help saying.

"I wasn't." Sebastian put his spoon down and gave James his full attention. "I panicked and did the only thing I could. How else would we have stopped that bear?"

James took Sebastian's hand. "I don't know. I'm not trying to blame you or tell you off for using the veins. It's not like we could have outrun it."

Parker frowned thoughtfully. "I could have tried to cut its throat with a knife from the diner's kitchen."

James was glad Parker hadn't tried anything that rash. He would have only hurt himself. "It was on fire."

"And already a corpse. Stabbing wouldn't have done anything when it was dead," Sebastian reminded them, though maybe Parker hadn't noticed that. James hadn't talked to him about the incident since bringing Sebastian home.

"We could have hit its eyes with light. Or fire." Parker shrugged as if in defeat. "I'm not saying I could have stopped it, but it'd probably pay to have some ideas up our sleeves in case that isn't the only possessed—or undead—animal to turn up."

"You're right." Sebastian rested a hand on James's thigh. "I can't keep doing this, but if I'm backed into another corner, it's not like I'm going to give up without fighting with everything I have."

"I know, sweetheart." James rubbed Sebastian's back. Hopefully, the next possessed animal wouldn't be a dead one, and they'd be able to deal with it without Sebastian's extra power, but the only way to guarantee something like this wouldn't happen again was to stop shades coming through the gateway.

After everyone had finished eating, Eli and Parker said goodbye and left.

James rinsed their bowls and put the rest of the soup away. "Do you have a headache?"

"No, it's okay at the moment. I'm just tired. I think I'll go back to bed."

James followed Sebastian back up to his bedroom.

Sebastian flopped on the bed, landing on his stomach. "I'm surprised Eli and Parker hung around all afternoon."

James lay beside him and rubbed his shoulders. "They care about you."

Sebastian turned his head to the side, propping it on a hand. "I'm not used to it. Every time Eli hugs me, it startles me." Sebastian rolled his eyes at himself. "Not in a bad way. I like being able to tell they care. It's just that the voice inside me that keeps asking *why* hasn't gone away yet."

James's heart ached at Sebastian's honesty. "It might take time for you to get used to the idea that they'll keep showing up for you."

"Yeah, probably. I can't hand out trust easily, no matter how good I know people are." Sebastian scooted closer and tucked his face into James's neck. "Except with you."

James kissed the top of Sebastian's head and murmured, "I'm glad I can be that person for you."

He didn't discount how much Sebastian opening up meant. James would have understood if it had taken longer for them to get to a fully trusting place, but he was glad he didn't have to wait. He was ready to build on that trust and keep Sebastian forever.

His visions of their future had grown exponentially since leaving Storm House. Sebastian made James want to be brave. He wanted to be there for Sebastian and not let his anxiety about losing people stand in the way. Yes, it had scared him when Sebastian lost consciousness today, but that fear wasn't going to make him hold back from connections like it used to.

"Wish we were at your house," Sebastian mumbled sleepily.

James looked down at him. "Why?"

Sebastian untucked himself from James. "I don't like this place."

James studied the bare room. "You might like it better once you make it yours."

Sebastian wrinkled his nose. "I don't want to make it mine."

"But you still want to live on your own, right?"

Sebastian thought for a moment. "Yeah. I want to spend every second with you, but I also want to build a normal life and…I don't know."

James smiled. "I want to spend every second with you, too, but it's not really practical."

"No." Sebastian matched his grin.

James wrapped one of Sebastian's curls around his finger. "What don't you like about the duplex?"

"It doesn't feel right. I think it's too small, maybe?" Sebastian chewed his lower lip. "Don't get me wrong, Storm House was too big and a way worse place to be, but I don't think I want to live here either."

"This could just be a temporary home that you stay in while you figure out what you want more permanently."

"True." Sebastian tucked back into James. "I hadn't thought of that. I guess there's no rush to figure out what I want. I don't need to stress so much about what comes next for me."

"No, there's no rush." James kissed his curls. "I'll be here with you as long as it takes for you to decide, whatever it ends up being."

"That feels really fucking good." Sebastian squeezed him. "Which is silly considering where I want to live and what I want to do with my time are far from my biggest problems."

"No, but they matter and will only matter more once all this is over. One problem doesn't discount all others. The veins aren't your whole life. It's good to look ahead."

Sebastian hummed a happy sound. "Something to look forward to."

JAMES AND ELI went to Storm House together the next morning, leaving Sebastian in bed. He woke briefly but told James he'd rather sleep than go look at the fuel cell with them. James was happy to let him rest. Sebastian hadn't had any more headaches, but there was no reason to push him when they didn't need extra help in the clearing.

The sun had gone, leaving clouds darkening the sky. When James and Eli reached the clearing, it seemed quiet. There weren't even birds pecking at the ground or flying between the trees. The fuel cell tilted to the side even more off-center than before.

Eli shrugged his backpack off. "Why is it falling over?"

"I don't know." James approached it as Eli went to uncover the mechanism closest to the path. "It's heavy, but I wouldn't think it'd sink into the earth due to its weight. The ground isn't exactly soft out here."

As he rounded the fuel cell, he stopped short and almost tripped. "What the hell?" The ground in front of the fuel cell—not visible from the path because it was on the opposite side of the large cylinder—opened into a hole.

James backed up.

Eli looked up from his notebook. "What's up?"

"Come over here, but be careful. Don't get too close to the fuel cell."

Eli approached. When he rounded the fuel cell, his mouth dropped open. "Where's my fifth mechanism?"

"What?" James looked around. The tarp-covered crate and

mechanism that had been next to the fuel cell were nowhere to be seen, just the hole and the fuel cell tilting toward it.

"Did it fall in?" Eli stepped forward.

James caught his arm. "Wait. What if the ground is unstable. It doesn't look like that hole was dug. There's no dirt around."

Eli moved back. "You think it's a sinkhole?"

James held Eli tight. "It must be."

The hole wasn't much bigger than the small missing crate. The fuel cell wasn't in danger of slipping in and disappearing unless the hole widened, but there was nothing to say that wouldn't happen.

Eli groaned. "It's eaten all my data from the last day."

James marveled at Eli's unwavering focus on studying and data. "I don't think that's the most important thing right now."

Eli ignored that. He probably disagreed. "We should look inside. What if the crate and everything is just under the surface. I could fish it out. It's not like it's a hole to the center of the earth."

James wasn't so sure. "Given it's a mysterious hole at the vein intersection, it could be anything."

Eli shrugged. "So tie a rope around me and let me get closer. We need to figure this out."

James wanted to say hell no, but Eli's suggestion was smart, and he had a point. They needed answers, and looking at the hole from five feet away wasn't giving them much.

They trooped off to the barn, saying hello to Miss Moo and checking her hay and water trough before returning to the clearing with a sturdy rope. James secured one end to a tree and the other to Eli. Maybe they were being overly cautious, but James was taking no unnecessary risks.

James held the coiled rope, giving Eli enough slack to get close to the hole.

He approached and peered down. "Okay, that's deep."

"How deep?"

"I can't see the bottom."

"Really?" James was shocked, despite his concern the hole could be something exactly like this.

"It's so dark." Eli leaned over the hole. "The ground feels fine next to it. Not unstable, at least in this spot. I don't see my mechanism." Eli turned and walked back to James.

James began removing the rope from Eli. "We should move the fuel cell. It's tied to the veins magically, but I don't want to lose sight of it."

Eli agreed.

The only way to move it was levitation. James performed the spell and shifted the fuel cell over toward the path. He didn't put it directly next to a mechanism in case another one got sucked into the ground. The fuel cell had drained more since they'd been here last, but the drop wasn't any bigger than the worst of what Eli and Parker had seen earlier that week.

"I have no idea why this would have happened," Eli said as he crouched over another crate, getting the data from across the clearing.

"Could it be because the intersection is a gateway?" James leaned against a tree to rest after doing the levitation spell. "How does that even work? I don't get how a gateway to Beyond can be underground."

"They always are. Veins are in the earth and shifting ones are no different. For shades, it doesn't matter. They can leave their solid form, move through the space between worlds created by the shifting energy, come out here, and return to solid form once they've moved through the ground to the surface."

James glared at the hole. "Could the ground be getting sucked through the gateway to Beyond?"

"I want to say no, that's never happened anywhere else that I've heard of, but this situation is pretty much unprecedented, so I have no idea."

Eli always liked facts or having data-based theories, but to James, the hole seemed exactly like things from this world falling through the gateway to Beyond.

6

SEBASTIAN

Sebastian got out of bed eventually. He showered and dressed, then decided to get out of the duplex.

Sometime while he'd been unconscious, a bunch of mail had arrived for him. He now had his debit card, a nice set of over-ear headphones, and a laptop. He synced the headphones to his cell phone and selected some music.

Sebastian went to the General Store to try out his debit card. He kept the headphones on and felt more relaxed, knowing no one would try to talk to him when he clearly couldn't hear them.

He took a muffin to the register and slipped the headphones around his neck when Carla looked up at him.

"Hi, Sebastian." She smiled brightly.

"Hey." He pulled out his card.

"Got your money, I see." She chuckled and scanned the muffin. "Glad things are back to normal. Wasn't sure if that darkness had scared you off."

"No, I really am a local."

"Must be." She handed him the muffin. "In that case, you probably know there's a trivia night at the diner every other Monday. And in case you're looking for a team, my boyfriend and I need all the help we can get. My sister joins us, but she always steers us wrong. If you want to come along, let me know." Carla looked at him expectantly.

The invitation took Sebastian by surprise, making his stomach churn. Back in college, he wouldn't have hesitated to say he was game, but socializing had become nerve-wracking. "Maybe. I don't really like busy events."

Carla nodded. "Fair enough. I'm sure I'll see you around here, anyway."

"Probably." He shrugged. "Have a good day."

At least Carla hadn't seemed annoyed by his response. She was very friendly and Sebastian did want his own friends outside James's group. Maybe they could do something else together other than trivia.

Sebastian took his muffin to the park. Maybe he should have been wary of the place after the bear incident, but he didn't think it any more likely a possessed animal would show up just because one had yesterday. He wasn't going to hide inside twenty-four-seven.

It felt good to get out and wander for no reason. He was still adjusting to everything not being trapped at Storm House entailed, and most of it was good. He appreciated sitting among the fall leaves, listening to music, and eating a sweet blueberry muffin more than he would have otherwise.

A man walking through town gave him a funny look before entering the diner. It gave Sebastian a flash of insecurity. Did he look weird or something?

He didn't have long to worry about it. James showed up a minute later. He'd dropped Eli at home and filled Sebastian in on their trip to his cursed property.

"Sounds like things are getting sucked into the gateway." Sebastian agreed with James's conjecture. "It must be connected to whatever I did to the veins, banishing the darkness."

James tensed next to him, saying quietly, "It feels like we have less and less time to figure this out."

"Yeah, everything's crumbling and getting less manageable by the day." Sebastian rubbed James's shoulders, ignoring the sinking feeling settling over him. "I think I should call my mom."

"What?" James's eyes widened in alarm.

"She might know more about how the imbalance started. Her dad was alive at the beginning of all this. Yeah, he was a little kid, but he had to have known something happened or had his own suspicions and insights about what his parents and grandmother were doing over the years. I have no idea how much he passed on to my mom and Uncle Stephen before he died. I'm not going to assume Stephen told me everything he knew."

James's frown cut deep lines around his mouth. "Do you think your mom will tell you if she knows anything?"

A surge of anger coursed through Sebastian. His mom had refused to help him before, in even the smallest ways. "I don't know. I can't make her talk, but I'm not above manipulating her if I have to. She'll be worried about Kira when she hears I've escaped. Maybe I can use that."

A muscle in James's jaw ticked. "Whatever you need to do, I'll support you."

Sebastian squeezed James's knee. His support meant everything. Sebastian pulled out his phone. He had his mom's number memorized unless she'd changed it in the last six years. Before he could think too hard about what talking to her would be like, he dialed and listened to it ring. The voicemail picked up, and he heard Samantha Storm's voice for the first time in years.

"Hi, it's Sebastian. Call me." He left his number and hung up.

Sebastian figured giving almost no information would be the best way to try and get his mom to respond. A nasty part of him wished he could see her face when she got that message. She'd be shocked at the very least, maybe even scared not knowing how Sebastian had contacted her.

James took Sebastian's hand. They sat for a few moments in silence before he said, "Eli wants to read over anything you have about the veins and any letters or notes you have from Selma, Sullivan, or Nelson."

Sebastian gripped the silent phone. "That's a good idea. Eli might catch something I missed. Hell, I might even read everything over again too. We've got nowhere else to look for answers."

"Eli and Parker are going out there again later this afternoon. If you have the letters and journals somewhere easy to find, they can grab them. Or I can go out and search."

"They're in a box in the library. I gathered up everything I could find and dumped it all together."

James unlocked his phone and began texting. "Great. I wasn't looking forward to searching for more papers, if I'm honest."

Sebastian snorted. "No, me either."

James tucked his phone away after he was done relaying everything to Eli.

"Have you heard anything from Eleanor and Hazel?" Sebastian asked.

James nodded. "They checked whether Eleanor was trapped yesterday. She's stuck behind the barrier with us. Hazel checked too, for good measure, and she's still trapped."

"I know it's what we expected, but dammit." Sebastian rubbed his temple as a twinge of pain started behind his eyes.

"Yeah," James agreed with a tired sigh. He stood from the bench and stretched. "What are you up to for the rest of the day?"

Sebastian got up. "I might go back to bed."

James put his hands on Sebastian's shoulders and looked him over. "Are you feeling okay?"

"My head aches a bit, and I'm tired." Walking one whole block to the park had worn him out. Sebastian needed to be careful with himself since he didn't know what the veins' power had done to him. If his body wanted sleep, he would listen and hope to have more energy when he woke again.

"You should eat something too." James took his hand and began walking back toward the duplex. "I'll bring some of the food Parker left at my place over to yours."

"Thanks, James." A breeze swept fallen leaves across the sidewalk that crunched under Sebastian's feet. "What're you going to do with the rest of your day?"

"I should probably go to work." James threw a sideways look at him and smiled.

Sebastian grinned back. "Yeah, you should. You've been lazy."

James shook his head, squeezing Sebastian's hand.

As they passed the bar on the corner of the town center, William came out of the post office across the street. He glared at them, making a sneering, degusted face before turning toward town hall.

"I really don't like that guy." Sebastian stared after him. "What was that look about?"

"I don't know. I've never liked him either."

Sebastian pushed William from his mind, trying not to let the strange look trigger his insecurity. He didn't need to dwell on the opinions of random people in town. He had bigger problems to deal with.

SEBASTIAN WOKE from his nap late that afternoon to a box of familiar papers in his living room. He heated up some of the lasagna James had brought over and emptied the box's contents on the table.

He started with Selma's journal and paid close attention to anything to do with her sons, but as he remembered, she hadn't recorded anything about the veins of power on their property.

She mentioned Nelson leaving and detailed her personal feelings on the abandonment but never touched on the root of her anger toward her son. *He'd ruined so much, taken something from them he could never replace, and broken their family.* But that was as close as Selma got to discussing the disaster with the veins.

Selma seemed more upset with Nelson than Sullivan. Perhaps she respected Sullivan for dealing with his mistake instead of running. Nelson was apparently greedy and overly ambitious. Though, years later, Selma wasn't complaining about that ambition when she demanded shares in Nelson Power. She felt he *owed* her, Sullivan, and the rest of the Storms, apparently.

None of it felt helpful.

The letters from Nelson to Selma and Sullivan were even worse. They were terse and as brief as possible. One just said: *No, it's not possible.* That was all. Sebastian suspected the letters to Nelson held more information, but he didn't have those. They'd probably been thrown out decades ago by whoever dealt with Nelson's estate after he passed away, if Nelson had even saved them.

Sebastian read and ate, moving on to pumpkin soup for his second course until he'd gotten through all the papers. He texted Eli to let him know he was done with them.

Just as Eli texted back to say he'd come pick the box up, there was a knock on Sebastian's door. He went to answer it and found James on his doorstep.

"How was your nap?" James kissed him on the cheek as he entered.

"Good. My head hasn't hurt since."

James nodded in approval. He picked up Selma's journal. "Find anything—" His question was cut off by the ringing of Sebastian's phone.

He grabbed it off the table. "It's my mom."

James was at his side in an instant. "I'm right here."

Sebastian wanted to say it was fine, but his stomach roiled. He gripped James's hand and accepted the call, switching it to speaker so James could listen in.

"Sebastian?" his mom asked when he didn't say anything, her voice hesitant like she didn't believe he was there.

He cleared his throat. "It's been a while."

There was a long silence. "How did you get a phone to work at the house?"

Not: how are you or are you okay? She went straight for the curse, wondering how Sebastian was getting around it.

Sebastian ground his teeth. "I'm not at the house."

The silence was even longer this time. "How?" The word came though full of fear. "Don't lie to me. Is this even really you calling? How would I know?"

"It's not like you'd recognize your son's voice or anything." Sebastian closed his eyes. It wouldn't pay to antagonize her too much, but he couldn't control himself. "In case you still aren't sure, it's me, the one you cursed to save your daughter. The one you left to get imprisoned after Stephen died. The one—"

"All right," she snapped. "Point made, Sebastian. Is this why you called? To shame your evil mother?"

"I need to know everything your dad told you about the curse and the veins."

"Why?" She waited for an answer, but Sebastian didn't give one. "How did you get away from the house without the area exploding? Something like that would have been in the news. You can't have escaped if there was no explosion."

"If you want to know how I got out, tell me about the curse and the veins."

"You haven't called your sister, have you?"

The words hit Sebastian like ice. "Why don't you ask her?" Sebastian was overwhelmed with bitterness. His sister had never asked for their mother's favor or been aware of what Sebastian had saved her from, but part of him hated her for being given all the affection he'd craved.

He hated his mom even more fiercely, in a way he thought he'd moved past years ago. Apparently not.

"Don't you dare try to tell Kira about any of this. She won't come visit you. You won't be able to trap her."

It hurt that his mother thought he'd do that, but it wasn't in his interest to correct her. She needed to feel threatened, or she'd never help. "If you want to guarantee that won't happen, talk to me."

"I don't know anything, Sebastian," she snapped.

"That's not what Stephen said. You knew about all of this." Sebastian took a breath, trying to calm down. "I think your dad knew what Sullivan and Nelson did. All I'm asking is that you tell me, and then you'll never hear from me again."

"Why does it matter? If you're free, why do you care?"

"Being free hasn't fixed anything. The curse is still here. It's just changing."

His mom sucked in a breath. "I have to go." She hung up.

Sebastian set the phone on the table with a shaking hand, and James pulled him into a tight embrace. "That won't be the end of it," he said into James's hair. "She's afraid of the curse. Once she checks on Kira, I'll hear from her again."

"Do you still think she knows something?"

Sebastian pulled back. "I have no idea, but she's the only one who would possibly have information. I have to rule it out and ensure she isn't hiding anything." He hated that figuring this out might all come down to his mother. She was the one who forced the curse on him, and it was hard to believe she'd help now, no matter how he tried to convince her. But he had to try.

SEBASTIAN FELT EVEN MORE needy than usual after the phone call with his mom. He didn't think he'd ever be unaffected by the abandonment he'd experienced at her hands, but he wasn't letting it dominate his life anymore. He had James, with whom he felt safe and secure, and it was okay for him to need comfort when things like this came up.

After Eli picked up the box, James took Sebastian to bed and showered him with kisses. He never held back affection, never did anything but accept Sebastian no matter what side of himself Sebastian showed.

"Is it weird that I need you to fuck me after that conversation?" Sebastian breathed into James's mouth as they kissed.

"No." James shifted his weight, looking down at Sebastian with a tender expression. "You need to know you're loved and cherished. That one person's rejection doesn't hold more weight than everyone else's choice to stand by you. That's all normal, sweetheart."

Sebastian blinked at James. "I—I'm loved?"

James's cheeks went dark red, but his gaze stayed soft. "Of

course you are, Sebastian. I didn't mean to say it so offhand the first time, but there's no doubt in my mind that I love you."

Sebastian wrapped his arms around James's neck. His heart skittered, and he smiled as warmth bloomed in his chest. "I love you too, James. I've been falling in love with you for so long." Sebastian clung to James, too many feelings coursing through him. "When I thought I'd lost you and would never get to see what that love would turn into, it broke me."

James let out a strangled sound. "I'm here," he promised, stroking Sebastian's cheek. "You didn't lose me. We're only at the beginning of our time together. You have so much love in your future, Sebastian. I know it."

A whine escaped Sebastian's throat. "Make love to me?" The request came out in a soft whisper, leaving Sebastian feeling more vulnerable than ever.

James kissed him, their tongues tangling. "There's nothing I want more, sweetheart."

Tears swam in Sebastian's eyes. He hadn't expected his feelings to be this intense. James loving him wasn't a total surprise. He hadn't expected to hear it this soon, but he'd known they were headed in that direction, so why did it change his world to hear those three words?

James ran his hands delicately over Sebastian's body in almost reverent movements. There was nowhere they hadn't touched each other, yet tonight, everything felt new.

Once they were naked, neither rushed toward getting off. They kissed and held each other, nothing but sweetness and love between them. Sebastian had been emotional during sex plenty of times, but not like this.

He sensed the same happening for James. It had been fun to see James embrace a new boldness and be overtly sexual as he opened up. This wasn't like that. There were no sexy words or thrillingly explicit requests. It was a new kind of open. James gave Sebastian all his deepest feelings, expressing his love and need for Sebastian even more powerfully than he had when he'd let loose and claimed him.

James kissed and licked Sebastian, tracing his throat and collarbone. Their cocks rubbed together in a sensual, unhurried rhythm.

"I love you," James breathed against Sebastian's shoulder.

Sebastian's skin tingled. He ran his fingers through James's hair. "I love you too."

James kissed down his body and licked Sebastian's cock from root to tip. He sucked on Sebastian's balls and spread him to kiss his hole. His tongue was soft, movements careful and thorough but no less pleasurable than the times he'd devoured Sebastian in a frenzy.

James grabbed the lube and began to open Sebastian while he kissed his thighs and sucked his cock. When Sebastian was ready, James pressed his bare cock to his hole, and Sebastian trembled. James looked down at him with so much affection that Sebastian couldn't breathe.

James pushed in. "Sweetheart," he gasped as he filled Sebastian in one measured thrust.

Sebastian remembered to breathe again, gasping, "James." He pulled him close and got lost in their kisses.

James's cock stretched him, the slide of skin on skin capturing Sebastian's attention. Each noise James made echoed in Sebastian's ears, imprinting itself in Sebastian's memory. Altogether, it was beautiful.

The slow rhythm of rocking hips and soft whines went on and on. Sebastian had never lasted this long. He never wanted this to end. James's cock dragged over Sebastian's prostate, and Sebastian moaned, but James kept it slow, letting Sebastian's pleasure build but never burst.

James pulled out and replaced his cock with his fingers. "I want you in my lap. I need to hold you every way I can."

"Yes." Sebastian sighed and clenched around James. He always wanted to be held.

James sat up against the pillows and headboard, pulling Sebastian onto him. Sebastian sank down on his cock and wrapped his arms around James as James cradled his waist. Sebastian rolled his hips and rubbed his nose against James's. He kept their sensual pace, wishing they could be connected like this forever.

"I love you, James."

James gasped and tightened his hold on Sebastian. "I love you too." He thrust up and shuddered, eyes locked on Sebastian's. "I'll always love you," he groaned desperately as his cock pulsed, coming and filling Sebastian.

Sebastian moaned, echoing James. His heart was so full. James's love was so clear that Sebastian couldn't have doubted it if he'd tried. They clung to each other, James letting out shuttering breaths as Sebastian worked his hips, dragging out James's orgasm and showing James his love was just as strong.

Sebastian stilled as James's orgasm faded. He didn't move off James, wanting to hold his release inside him and be filled by James's cock as long as possible. James grasped Sebastian's aching, precum-slick dick, stroking in firm, tender motions that matched the rest of their lovemaking. He kissed Sebastian deep, accepting Sebastian's whimpers into his mouth as Sebastian began to come at last.

James whined as Sebastian clenched around his sensitive cock. Sebastian's orgasm seemed to roll on in waves and left him completely spent, held tight in James's arms.

Sebastian had no doubts, fears, or reservations when it came to James.

They were in love.

JAMES

James and Sebastian showered together once they summoned the willpower to get out of bed. James found himself in a drowsy, deeply satiated state. He couldn't stop smiling.

"I've never been this happy," he murmured into Sebastian's ear.

"Me either." Sebastian dropped his head back and James kissed down his neck, chasing the water droplets cascading down his sweet skin.

A loud bang came from somewhere in the house. They both stilled, catching each other's eye.

Sebastian frowned. "That didn't sound like someone knocking on the door."

"No." James rinsed the remaining soap from his body and they got out of the shower.

Sebastian passed him a towel. "Things have remained quiet on the shade front, right?"

"As far as I've heard, yeah." There weren't any more noises, and James wondered if they were being overly cautious. Could it have been a car backfiring or something on the neighbor's side of the building?

They dried quickly and exited the bathroom. James needed to start keeping some clothes here. He pulled on his discarded boxer briefs as Sebastian peered out the window.

It was fully dark. James had no idea what time it was. They'd made love for what felt like hours. He wished the reality of their situation hadn't intruded so quickly. He'd wanted the rest of the night to bask in soft, tender feelings with Sebastian.

"There are shades in the town circle," Sebastian said, not looking away from the window.

James hurried up behind him. "Are there a lot?" Over Sebastian's shoulder, he could see about a dozen flying around the street and above the stone monument in the middle of the town square.

"Doesn't seem too bad." Sebastian hesitated. "Unless more are coming."

James placed a hand on the small of Sebastian's back, rubbing his thumb over the dimples he loved so much. "At least they aren't swarming the duplex. I was afraid that sound was one hitting a window."

"Me too."

A shade popped up out of nowhere, directly on the other side of the glass, and banged its fists against it, making them both jump.

"Shit." James took a deep breath as his heart pounded. It was almost like the shade had heard him and chosen that moment to pounce.

"It's the one wearing my robe." Sebastian pointed, mouth open in outrage. Sure enough, dirty purple sleeves hung around the shade's elbows, the robe half falling off its shoulders.

The shade swooped away.

Sebastian turned to face James. "What the fuck?"

He shrugged. "I have no idea."

"It's taunting me." Sebastian turned back to the window, but the shade was no longer in sight.

James bent to pick up Sebastian's underwear and handed it to him. "It would be funny that it still has your robe if we weren't having such serious shade problems."

"Yeah, hilarious. It's annoying, is what it is." Sebastian pulled his boxer briefs on. "We should probably keep an eye on them even if they aren't trying to break in."

"Good idea." James pulled on the rest of his clothes. "Why don't I go downstairs and get some food, and we can watch them out the window?"

Sebastian agreed and perched on the bed to watch the shades swooping around outside.

James brought dinner up. They turned out the lights in the bedroom and watched the shades as they ate. The beasts didn't seem to be doing anything like the dancing around the stone Sebastian had seen before the darkness from Beyond had set in, and most of the streetlights still hadn't been repaired, so even their presence in town wasn't too far out of the ordinary, given how dark it was.

The only thing James could glean from the spectacle was that shades were back in Moonlight Falls, and it hadn't taken long. Sebastian had banished almost all of them when he'd saved James and defeated the darkness. How many shades might be out on Sebastian's property streaming through the gateway right this moment? James was glad he wasn't there to find out.

THE NEXT MORNING, James slipped out of bed without waking Sebastian and got ready for work. He and Hazel had a lot to do. It had been hard to prioritize the electrical business over the last week with the vein problem looming over them and not knowing if Sebastian would recover. Now that they knew Sebastian was all right, they had to get going on replacing the busted lights in town.

James was downstairs making coffee when Sebastian joined him. He'd wrapped up in a hoodie and gray sweatpants, his hair tousled. He looked absolutely adorable.

Sebastian gave James a sleepy smile. "Thought I smelled coffee."

James handed him a mug. "Sorry if I woke you." They'd been up late watching the shades. It had been after midnight when the beasts had flown away. James hoped they hadn't been off to do anything destructive.

"It's fine." Sebastian spooned powdered creamer into his mug. "I'll go back to bed if I need to. I'm not too tired, or I wouldn't have gotten up."

James pulled him in for a kiss. "Okay. Good." He buried his nose in the hair behind Sebastian's ear and let himself relax, feeling nothing but love.

Someone knocked on the door.

Sebastian pulled away and went to open it. James followed, finding Eli on the doorstep holding a familiar box.

"Hey, Eli." Sebastian stepped out of the way. "Have you finished with the papers already?"

"Yeah." Eli walked past Sebastian and set the box on the table. "I texted you saying I was coming by." He looked at James.

"Must have missed it." James returned to the kitchen and grabbed a third mug from the cupboard.

Sebastian drifted toward the coffee, and Eli joined them.

"Anything catch your eye when reading?" Eli asked Sebastian.

"No, it was about as I remembered." Sebastian poured coffee from the French press into his mug. "I've wondered if whatever happened had to do with Nelson and his quest to unlock the secrets of harnessing natural power, but there was nothing in the papers to confirm it."

James explained to Eli who Nelson Storm was in relation to Nelson Power.

Eli's brows raised. "You think a failed experiment caused the imbalance?"

"Yeah." Sebastian shrugged. "But I have no idea what they would have done or how it broke things, if that's what happened. Selma felt Nelson owed the family when his company took off, but that could just be her expecting compensation for their suffering and not because the vein disaster had anything to do with his later inventions."

"It would make sense if whatever happened in the clearing was a failed early experiment," Eli said as he helped himself to coffee. "Maybe when Selma referenced Nelson taking something he could never replace, she meant taking something from the veins rather than from the family."

James considered Eli's words. "What can you take from a vein other than raw energy?"

"Maybe that's what he took?" Eli gave James a pointed look. "Magical power plants take energy from veins and convert it into electricity, but safely. What if the Storm brothers took energy, but doing it wrong caused an explosive imbalance?"

"And Selma's been trying to put the energy back with the curse ever since." Sebastian closed his eyes briefly. "If that's the case, it doesn't seem like the energy can be replaced permanently. No amount seems to fill the void."

There was a grim silence.

If this was the answer to what happened to the veins, James didn't see how it'd helped them fix it.

"How can taking a finite amount of energy out of a system create an infinite debt?" James scowled at the idea that natural laws could be broken like that. "It's magic, but it still needs to add up. Whatever they may have taken couldn't result in a negative larger than the original amount."

"I'd agree." Eli put a hand on James's arm, probably sensing his frustration. "But we don't understand veins as well as we understand how other magical energy exchanges work. Maybe different laws govern magic flowing between worlds. If so, we have no idea what energy getting trapped permanently in our world would result in."

James had never considered taking energy out of a vein as trapping it in this world. Vein energy constantly moved between worlds, whether through the whole vein as it did in shifting formations or at the end of fixed formations. Trapping energy in the human world and not letting it flow between could very well do more than deprive the vein of whatever amount of energy was taken.

Sebastian seemed to study Eli. "Even if they took energy, that doesn't tell us how to solve it. Putting energy back clearly isn't a permanent solution, and I don't know if Nelson Power's secret method of safely extracting energy is our answer either. If that were the case, why didn't Nelson come home and fix things permanently and free his brother?"

"Maybe we're wrong." Eli drained his coffee and set his empty mug down on the counter. "Maybe they didn't take energy. Remember, whatever's happening at the intersection is causing higher energy levels than what we're seeing in town. I'm not sure how taking energy would have that result, even if we don't know what trapping it in this world would do."

Defeat hung in the air as Eli left. He'd promised to spend the day researching all possibilities, looking for answers on what happened to veins when energy was taken or why vein energy levels might rise.

Sebastian abandoned his mostly untouched coffee. "What if we can't solve this?" James sensed the beginning of panic in his words. "What if there was never an answer, and the only way was leaving Selma's curse and the veins alone?" He gave James a hard look. "What if I ruined everything by using the veins to banish the darkness and I destroyed the precarious balance we had. What if it's all downhill from here until it ends in disaster?"

James took Sebastian's trembling hands. "You didn't ruin anything when you used the veins. You saved the town. Maybe things wouldn't have become this unstable if you hadn't beat the darkness, but not banishing it would have been worse. People would have died. *We* would have died. The invasion might have spread past Moonlight Falls. And for all we know, the spell the shades cast on the veins is what fucked everything up, not you using the veins' energy to save us."

"I guess it doesn't matter. It's done now, regardless." Sebastian gave a tired sigh. "We have to deal with the situation either way. I just can't get rid of my guilt."

"You have nothing to feel guilty for."

"I know. I'm trying to remember that. It's just hard." Sebastian gave James a small smile. "Your reassurance always makes me feel better."

James returned his smile. "Then it's a good thing I'm here to remind you."

"Yeah." Sebastian's attention landed on the box of old papers. "I should call my lawyer and see if I can get any useful information on Nelson Power, seeing as I own a good portion of the company, just in case Nelson held the key to stabilizing the vein after all. Who knows, Nelson might have known how to save his family and chosen not to."

"Maybe taking energy out of the vein safely will bring everything back into balance," James mused. It was a long shot, but it would be silly not to try and test it. They couldn't afford to leave any possibility unexplored.

JAMES WENT to Gray Electrical to meet Hazel and get started on replacing the lights in town. They loaded everything they needed into Hazel's new van and drove the short distance to the town circle.

Hazel pulled over in front of the first broken light. "Eleanor asked if we'd have much warning before things explode, but I told her I had no idea."

James got out of the van and helped Hazel unload the new light and a ladder. "We might not have much warning, but if things get worse, like if the energy in the fuel cell drops too much or the weird sinkhole gets much bigger, maybe we should get everyone out of here."

Hazel nodded in agreement. "Better to be on the safe side."

They fixed the lights on the diner side of the circle, and Parker came out periodically to ward them. Around midday, Sebastian met them for lunch in the park, and they all dug into Parker's club sandwiches, Sebastian with a vegetarian version.

James wanted to enjoy the moment. He had his friends and the man he loved. He wanted to daydream about last night and get caught up in picturing his future and all the ways he and Sebastian's love for each other could grow.

But he couldn't. The uncertainty of the veins hung over everything like a dark cloud. James had never been so scared the future he wanted would be taken from him. It was the same old fear that had always plagued him, causing him to shy away and detach himself, but he wouldn't stay that way this time. He wanted to fight. He wouldn't let anything come between him and Sebastian. He just wished he knew how to save them.

As they finished eating, James spotted William exiting town hall. He crossed the street, heading toward them, glaring.

"Great, just what we need," he grumbled, and Hazel grunted in agreement.

William fixed his attention on Sebastian as he reached the picnic table. "You should have stayed at your haunted house."

Sebastian's eyes widened in shock.

"Excuse me?" James snapped. That comment was unnecessarily aggressive, even for William, who was always antagonistic. Why did he care that Sebastian lived in town these days?

William ignored James, continuing to glare at Sebastian like he couldn't stand to be near him. "You Storms have ruined this town. Put all of us at risk."

James froze. At risk? Wait, what? Did William know something? How? Eleanor never would have told him about the veins.

Sebastian's hand shook where it rested on James's knee. "What are you talking about?"

William huffed. "I know there's a ticking timebomb on your property, and we all might die now that you've abandoned your post and come into town." He eyed them all smugly as if he'd just proven his anger was beyond reproach.

James stood from the table. He was reeling, wondering *how*, but the need to defend Sebastian was stronger. William knew something, but he had it all wrong. "That isn't true. Sebastian being in town hasn't put anyone at risk."

"No? I heard you all talking to Eleanor." William turned away from Sebastian to sneer at James. "You're always turning up, poking your noses into official business you have no right to. I figured I'd see what you were up to this time. Turns out it was worse than I thought. Eleanor is trying to cover up your mistakes. She's been sneaking around frantically trying to access all kinds of things she should need extra approval for."

"You listened at her office door?" Hazel asked, her disgust clear.

"I shouldn't have had to. It was lucky I saw you three creeping into town hall." William stood up straighter, crossing his arms. "Eleanor can't seriously believe it isn't the Storms' fault we all might blow up. Of course you'd frame it like you were a victim, Sebastian, to take the heat off you. Only someone gullible would take your word for it. Eleanor knew the rest of the city council wouldn't stand for your nonsense, so she's keeping us in the dark. Instead of taking charge, she's *helping* you. Covering her ass as well as yours." He jabbed a pointed finger at Sebastian.

Sebastian's cheeks turned red. "Didn't you hear me warning Eleanor? There's a good reason she isn't telling anyone, and it has nothing to do with sneaking around or covering anything up. This isn't just about the unstable veins on my property. There's a curse—"

"As if *hearing* something could trap me," William scoffed. "What a pathetic excuse. I bet you made that up to try and keep what you've done from getting out."

James took a step toward William. Of course he didn't believe the warning. *Shit*. Had he not stuck around to hear Eleanor's failed attempt to report the veins to the officials? "You haven't told anyone else, have you?"

William turned up his nose. "People have a right to know."

James's heart sank.

"For fuck's sake, William," Parker growled. "You're a fool. You've trapped anyone you've told."

"No." William spat back, full of aggression, even though his confident expression wavered. "That's ridiculous. If anyone's trapping people, it's him." He pointed at Sebastian again.

Hazel got up from the bench and pulled out her phone. She walked across the street, making a call before James could ask if she was going to find Eleanor.

"Since no one is doing anything about this disaster, I've called a meeting," William went on. "You Storms need to be dealt with."

Sebastian looked stunned, blinking like he didn't know how to respond. James went to his side, resting a hand on his shoulder. They didn't need this. It was bad enough stressing about finding a solution without ignorant pain-in-the-asses causing even more problems.

Parker rounded the table and grabbed William by the arm. "Don't tell anyone else. Do you hear me? This isn't ridiculous. It's dead serious." He used every bit of his stature and thundering voice to their full, intimidating potential, looming over William with anger in his eyes.

"Get off me." William pulled away, but worry finally broke through his arrogant expression. He hesitated, opened his mouth as if to say something, then turned and walked away without another word.

"Think he's off to test whether he's trapped?" Sebastian asked in a subdued voice.

"Why don't I go see?" Parker walked after the man. He turned and called over his shoulder, "I'll follow him and make sure he doesn't spread the secret to anyone else."

"And the people he's already told about Storm House?" James asked, even though he didn't expect Parker to know what to do about them.

Parker only grimaced before hurrying to follow William.

"This is bad," Sebastian whispered.

He could say that again. The people William had told wouldn't have any inkling that learning about the potentially explosive veins had consequences. Who knew how much further the Storm House secret had spread or how many people were now trapped.

THE AUDITORIUM at town hall was packed with people for William's meeting. Everyone there was trapped thanks to the man's big mouth and bullheadedness.

Sebastian's anxiety was at an all-time high, but he'd had no choice but to come. He couldn't hide at home while people discussed him and his family's curse. He couldn't pretend that their being stuck had nothing to do with him, even if he hadn't created this particular mess.

James stood shoulder to shoulder with him, but even that wasn't helping calm him.

Parker and Eleanor had stopped William from telling anyone else that afternoon. Too bad the damage had already been done. Everyone in the room had been told about the veins by William or someone he'd told, and none of them would be able to evacuate if it came down to the worst-case scenario.

Sebastian felt sick. As if the stakes for fixing the veins hadn't been high enough already. He'd tried calling his mom again, desperate for any new information. She hadn't answered. They were no closer to solving this than before, and everything seemed hopeless.

Eleanor stood on a small stage at the front of the auditorium. She looked livid. Sebastian would have been terrified to face her if he hadn't known she was on his side.

"Quiet," Eleanor barked, and the crowd stilled. "William, get up here and explain what you've done." She pointed to the stage beneath her feet, summoning him like he was about to get another verbal thrashing.

Hazel had told Sebastian how Eleanor had exploded at William that afternoon. Apparently, it hadn't been pretty. Eleanor had then dragged William to the barrier and showed him the reality of his situation. Sebastian was glad he hadn't been there for it.

William approached the stage with as much arrogance as ever. If he was concerned about being trapped, he wasn't showing it now. "It has come to my attention that we've all been cursed by the Storms," he announced.

People in the crowd made noises of confusion and alarm. Sebastian tried unsuccessfully to push away the guilt that had grown inside him all afternoon.

"No," Eleanor said sharply. "*You've* spread the curse, William. *You* have cursed these people." She turned her attention to the crowd. "All of you have learned about the veins of power on the Storm property, which have been at risk of explosion for decades, but what William failed to convey is that the knowledge comes with a curse..."

As Eleanor spoke, people turned to stare at Sebastian. Some looked shocked, others angry. Sebastian's pulse pounded in his ears. He wanted to sink into the wall behind him. Anxiety tightened in his chest until he felt like he couldn't breathe. He needed to get out of there.

He didn't move. He couldn't run from this, no matter what it was doing to him. This wasn't his fault, but he had to face it and try to help.

Parker, Eli, and Hazel stood next to him and James. He wished he found more comfort in that. They were on his side just like they'd promised, but everything about the situation was still hard to face.

"What are we going to do?" someone in the crowd called once Eleanor finished explaining.

"He never should have left his land," someone else shouted. "Things were fine for years. Put him back. This is all the Storms' fault."

There was a chorus of agreement.

Sebastian wondered if he was going to be sick. His head spun. Everyone hated him. They blamed him. They wanted to imprison him to solve their problems. This meeting was all his worst fears combined. No one in Moonlight Falls wanted him.

"He's not going anywhere," James said from beside Sebastian. "That's not going to fix anything, and even if it would have, this is not his fault, and he shouldn't be punished for it. William trapped you, not Sebastian."

Voices rose up on all sides of them.

Sebastian closed his eyes. He just wanted to live here and have a normal life, but that was never going to happen, was it?

"Enough," Eleanor shouted from the front of the room. Sebastian opened his eyes to see her glaring at the crowd. "William is the only one at fault here. He let his ignorance and arrogance put you all at risk."

"Fuck you, Eleanor," William sneered.

She might as well not have heard him. "Anyone who spreads this curse from here will face legal repercussions. Including you." She looked down her nose at William. "We're doing everything we can to solve the issue with the veins. There is no immediate risk of a disaster, so I urge everyone to stay calm."

"Why aren't you trying to solve the problem by putting someone back at Storm House?" a man near the front asked. "What are you actually doing? Shouldn't that be the first logical step?"

Most of the people in the room didn't know the full extent of the problem. They thought Sebastian leaving his property had caused things to deteriorate. They didn't know that the incident with the darkness was what had made things more unstable.

"We could trap William at Storm House and see how that goes," Eleanor suggested, though Sebastian got the impression she meant it sarcastically.

William lunged for her.

Eleanor cast a spell, pushing William back with a gust of wind before he could reach her. "Don't you dare."

He blustered, red in the face, but he didn't come for her again.

People in the crowd were murmuring their agreement with Eleanor's suggestion, but they were past trapping people to calm the veins.

"It won't help," Sebastian said so quietly he figured only James could hear him. "It won't help," he repeated, louder this time. "Me leaving the property didn't make it any more likely the veins would explode."

All eyes fixed on him. Sebastian's mind went momentarily blank. The stress of the situation seemed to be crushing him.

"Then what are you going to do?" someone asked.

"We're fixing the veins," Eli announced, stepping forward with an air of calm authority. "The veins need to be restored to their normal state. It's the only way to permanently stop the explosion. So unless any of you happen to have in-depth knowledge on the topic, we don't need more suggestions."

"That's right," Eleanor said, recapturing everyone's attention. "This meeting was only meant to alert you to what William omitted when telling you about the situation and to ensure this doesn't escalate further. Any other concerns can be brought directly to me."

"I still don't think he should be walking around free, like he didn't have a hand in all this," William couldn't seem to help saying, pointing at Sebastian. "You're blaming me for something I didn't start."

"If Sebastian hadn't been walking around free, we'd all still be in darkness or killed by shades by now," Eleanor snapped. "He saved this town."

No one seemed overly impressed or like they were going to accept Sebastian based on the mayor's words. Perhaps they didn't believe her. More than a few people eyed him suspiciously like they were keen to drag him back to Storm House to see if it solved their problems.

Sebastian had been cast out. He was back on the outside of Moonlight Falls, just as he had been as a child.

"Eleanor's right," James said, arm wrapping protectively around Sebastian. "We all owe Sebastian for banishing the beasts and dark magic from Beyond back to where they belong. Now, if you'll excuse us, I don't think anything else productive will come out of this meeting."

James guided Sebastian out. Parker, Hazel, and Eli followed.

Sebastian was shaking. He wished the town's rejection and anger didn't hurt him, but it did. It made him feel disposable. His own mother had treated him that way for so long that being cast aside felt like a permanent part of who he was. This would always happen.

But this time, he wasn't alone. He had James standing firmly by him, and when Sebastian focused on that, his world shifted. Not all people were good or understanding, and Sebastian couldn't change that. Not everyone was going to like him or believe him, but the important people would. James would. Eli, Parker, and Hazel would. Eleanor would.

He could have a life full of people who loved and cared about him. The anger of the rest of the town couldn't take that away.

The only thing that could ruin it all was the veins. They could take the lives of everyone he loved and cared for, the town, and all the people in that room. He had to stop the worst from coming to fruition. He could make good things happen and have faith they would last. For James. For their life together. For everyone who stood with him and even for the scared, angry people in town hall.

Not for William though. Screw that guy to the ends of the earth and back.

JAMES

JAMES LED Sebastian out of town hall, his blood boiling. How could any of them blame Sebastian when William was the problem?

He didn't let go of Sebastian as the group hovered on the sidewalk in the late afternoon light. "I'm so sorry you had to hear that."

Sebastian shifted in his arms. "It's all right, James."

"No, it's not. Even if they're scared, they shouldn't have placed blame on you."

"I don't think fear was why William was blaming me," Sebastian muttered.

Parker huffed. "No, that's just how he is. He'd blame anyone to avoid admitting he was wrong."

A few people exited town hall behind them, not stopping to say anything as they hurried to cars parked down the street.

"Want to head over to the diner for some food?" Parker asked the group.

James looked at Sebastian, making it clear it was up to him.

"That sounds good." Sebastian smiled, though James could make out worry lines around his eyes. "I'm an anxious mess from that meeting, but surely the diner is quiet enough at this time of day that I'll be able to calm down, and it won't make things worse."

"It should be. It's too early for most people to be going for dinner." James was surprised Sebastian had mentioned anything about being uncomfortable in the diner in front of the others. He must be finding it easier to trust them.

Parker led the way across the street, Eli and Hazel following closely. Several deer lurked at the back of the park as they passed, standing among the trees edging the grass where part of the forest came into town. No other people were around, and sure enough, the diner was almost deserted when they entered.

Luna, one of the longtime servers, greeted them and handed James a stack of menus. They picked a booth by a window, and James slid in next to Hazel so Sebastian could sit on his other side and not be boxed in. He seemed more relaxed as he settled next to James than he'd been in the town hall. No surprise there. It had been a tense situation regardless of social anxiety. Sebastian had handled it well.

Sebastian absently ran his fingers over the ear pads of his headphones, which he wore around his neck. He'd started bringing them any time he left the house. When James had met him in the park yesterday and he'd been wearing them, he'd looked happy and at ease, not to mention cute, with the ear covers poking out of his messy ginger curls.

They ordered and didn't have to wait long for their food. As they ate, everyone remained subdued. The silence wasn't necessarily bad. It made sense they were all in their heads with the mound of problems growing around them. James figured Sebastian might be appreciating the quiet. He sat pressed close to James, the physical contact clearly comforting.

James watched the deer out the window. It wasn't too surprising they'd stuck around since the park was empty, but when more showed up at the edge of the woods, James began to wonder. Was he being paranoid, or was this way more deer than were usually in town? They weren't eating the grass in the park either, just standing around.

"What are you staring at?" Sebastian asked, leaning forward to see around James.

"There's a bunch of deer in the park."

Eli narrowed his eyes from across the table. "Why does it feel like they're waiting for something?"

He was right. The animals had gone unnaturally still. Just as James was about to voice his agreement, a large stag walked out of the forest. It passed through the group of unmoving deer and marched onto the sidewalk. It looked up and down the street, head turning in a slow sweep from side to side.

Hazel put her iced tea down. "That can't be normal."

"At least they're not bears," Sebastian muttered.

James tried to get a good look at the deer's eyes but it was too difficult from inside. The longer he watched, the more sure he was that the deer were possessed. The stag on the sidewalk stood there as if it were looking for something, scanning the street periodically.

Sunset wasn't too far away. James was surprised shades would possess animals to come into town this late in the day. Why not just wait until dark?

Someone exited the General Store and walked down the sidewalk in their direction. The stag turned toward them and stomped its hooves, tossing its head, formidable antlers swinging through the air. The person stopped and took a tentative step backward.

"Should we go out and help?" Eli asked.

Banishing these shades should be easier than the one in the bear. At least the deer were alive.

"You might want to wait in here," Parker said gently, a hand on Eli's forearm. James agreed. Eli didn't need to face off with any possessed animals when he had no magic.

"Are we going to have to kill them?" Sebastian cringed like he hated to even think about it.

James wasn't much happier about the prospect. "They haven't tried to hurt anyone. Though that stag could run someone through easily enough."

They all hesitated. Trying to banish shades without killing their host was often not very successful. It was too hard to get them to leave the bodies.

The person on the sidewalk hurried back the way they'd come. James hoped the deer would move on but also didn't like the idea of a bunch of possessed animals wandering around unchecked.

"Eleanor's heading over." Hazel pointed out the window to where the mayor was crossing the circle.

Eleanor reached the stone and hesitated, clearly spotting the odd group of deer. Parker stood and Hazel nudged James with her elbow, prompting him to get out of her way.

It was a standoff. Eleanor on the grass, the stag on the sidewalk, and James, Sebastian, Hazel, and Parker hovering inside. The stag tossed its head.

Eleanor took a step backward.

"We can't let the deer scare everyone off." James took a decisive step toward the door. "And we can't just hide in here forever. We either need to banish the shades or scare them all back into the woods."

A car drove up the street, moving between Eleanor and the stag. She took the opportunity to move farther away, placing the stone between her and the beast. The stag stomped its hooves and charged after the car as if angered by the interruption. It rammed the back bumper with its antlers, and the car sped off.

James exited the diner with everyone but Eli close behind. The stag turned away from the car toward Eleanor. It stomped its hooves again. Was it targeting her specifically as a leader like the humanoid shade had?

It lowered its head like it was getting ready to charge. James summoned a ball of bright light and sent it racing toward the stag, straight into its eyes. The animal reared up on its back legs, letting out a cry of confusion. James kept the light in its face, forcing it to make contact with the stag, trying to get it in its eyes.

The shade shrieked, the unnatural sound coming from the stag's mouth. To James's horror, the stag had sharp onyx teeth.

Hazel rushed to Eleanor as Parker sent another ball of light at the stag's face, ushering it into the stag's open mouth. The stag thrashed, then froze as the light forced its way deeper inside. Black wisps of shadow flowed from its fur and burst into nothing.

James and Parker let their lights go out. The stag blinked and took off, running toward the forest like a scared animal, no longer possessed. The rest of the possessed deer melded back into the woods, probably not wanting to stick around and be banished back to Beyond.

Eleanor approached the group, Hazel at her side. "I'm glad that worked."

"Me too." James stared at the now-empty park. He hadn't wanted to kill a bunch of deer, but maybe that was why the shades had chosen them as their hosts.

Sebastian stared off in the same direction. "What do you think they were doing?"

"Who knows." Parker joined them in scrutinizing the trees as if they had answers. "They definitely seemed to be up to something."

"Regrouping for another attack on the town?" James suggested.

No one responded, but everyone had matching grim expressions as if they all feared the same.

"Why don't you come inside and get something to eat?" Hazel slung her arm through Eleanor's and the two women disappeared inside the diner.

James was about to suggest they follow when he noticed Sebastian's attention had shifted to the stone, a deep furrow in his brow. "What are you thinking?"

Sebastian crossed his arms. "There's something about this rock."

Eli, who'd come out of the diner when the deer fled, came to stand next to Sebastian. "Like what?"

"I swear it was glowing when the shade was preparing for its sacrifice. And when I was fighting off the darkness, it seemed like it exploded with light." Sebastian shook his head. "Does it have magic?"

James frowned at the tall stone. "It's just a rock, isn't it? A symbol?"

Sebastian turned to face him. "But the shades dancing around it before the darkness set in had to be them doing magic. It all centered around the stone. Why do that if it's just a rock?"

"It is strange now that I think about it," Eli said as he wandered closer to the stone. "It's right above a vein, but I've always thought it was just a rock too."

Parker came up behind Eli. "Can you check using your instruments to see if it has any magic of its own?"

"I can try." Eli bit his lip like he did when he was thinking hard.

"Maybe we should ward it," James suggested. "Sebastian's right. Shades dancing around it had to mean something, even if they were using the veins to create the darkness and it's nothing but a convenient rock."

"It wouldn't hurt," Parker agreed. "I need to eat some more and rest before doing another ward since I've already done a few today."

"Yeah, I don't want you straining yourself." Eli turned away from the stone, looking at Parker with concern.

"You'll look after me." He smiled down at Eli, and the two headed back into the diner.

James turned to follow when someone called out, "Sebastian!" He turned to find the librarian, Mila, waving at them from across the street.

Sebastian grabbed James's arm. "Was she in the meeting?"

"I didn't see her, but it was crowded. She could have been up near the front." From where Mila stood, it looked like she'd just come out of town hall.

"Shit." Sebastian set off across the street at a hurried pace, pulling James along.

11

SEBASTIAN

SEBASTIAN APPROACHED Mila in front of town hall, James at his side. Maybe he should have forced himself to stay as the meeting let out to get a better look at who was there. If he'd known Mila had been among the crowd, he'd have gone to her.

"I've been trying to talk sense into people," she said by way of greeting.

Sebastian stopped short. "What?"

Mila shook her head at him like she used to when he was young. "Come on, let's talk in the library. I closed up early, but I don't want to do this out here." She waved them over to the library entrance and unlocked the door.

Sebastian and James followed her inside. Half the lights were off, making the place dim and shadowy.

"You were at the meeting?" James asked.

Mila nodded grimly before turning to Sebastian. "Why don't you tell me the real story. I imagine I've only heard the smallest part."

Sebastian collapsed into a chair at a nearby table. "Who told you?"

Mila sat across from him. "My neighbor. She said there were

veins of power out at Storm House set to explode because you abandoned watching over them. I wanted to tell her it was nonsense, but…" Hurt and fear lined Mila's face. "Was that really the reason you were out there?"

Sebastian explained everything. He felt like he was getting more efficient at telling the tale after so many repeats, not that it made it easier in this case.

"Stephen," Mila whispered once Sebastian had explained the curse and how it passed through his family. She covered her mouth with a trembling hand, then lowered it, balled into a tight fist. "That's why he never gave us a chance to be together. What a stubborn fool."

"I'm sorry?" Sebastian glanced sidewise at James. It wasn't exactly what he'd expected her to say.

"According to you, Stephen's parents and grandparents had families and fairly full lives even with this curse. Why couldn't Stephen have done that? Why not let me in? I'd have worked through a relationship with him even if he never left the house. Even if I didn't know why. He didn't have to be there alone."

Sebastian didn't know how to answer.

"He must not have seen it that way," James said gently.

"Apparently." Mila sighed. "I suppose I don't know exactly what I would have done. Maybe I wouldn't have wanted to work through it, not knowing what he was hiding. I'll never get the chance to find out." She paused, shaking her head. "I can understand Stephen not wanting to have children given the curse, and who knows, maybe he never wanted a family. I just don't know what to think now. I went through my whole adult life not knowing half of what was happening between me and him."

Mila stared off into space for a long moment. Sebastian let her process, wondering if learning this was harder than thinking Stephen had rejected her and pushed her away due to his reclusive tendencies.

The librarian shook herself, looking at Sebastian and James

almost like she'd forgotten they were there. "I'm so glad you got out of there, Sebastian. You poor thing."

"I just wish it had ended when I left Storm House," Sebastian admitted.

"Of course, but your leaving didn't really make things more likely to explode, did it?"

Sebastian explained the rest of the story and how the darkness had impacted everything. "I'm sorry you've gotten sucked in. I hate to think that if we can't solve this, you won't be able to get out of town."

Mila waved him away like it was a minor inconvenience. "No need to be sorry. Not everything falls on you. And honestly, even if the worst happens, understanding why my past was the way it was is worth it. Something always nagged at me about Stephen, and now I know why. I can make peace and move on."

"I'm glad you see it that way." Something loosened in Sebastian's chest. He still hated that this could get Mila killed after everything she'd done for him, but he was glad she could find peace in the situation.

They hugged, and Sebastian relaxed even more. It felt good not to have secrets between them. They could rebuild their relationship in a more meaningful way now than if Sebastian was stuck lying forever.

They said goodnight, and Sebastian promised to see Mila again soon and keep her updated.

James took Sebastian back to his house rather than the duplex. Eli and Parker weren't there when they arrived, and despite the early hour, Sebastian was more than happy to retreat to James's room.

Perched on the edge of the bed, Sebastian tried calling his mom again. He called three times in a row to see if annoying her prompted her to pick up. It didn't. He thought about calling Kira just to rile everyone up, but he didn't have her number. It'd been over ten years since he'd seen or spoken to his sister. He never saw her or his mom again after moving in with Stephen permanently. He'd spoken to his mom periodically, but never Kira. She could be married with kids for all he knew.

Sebastian flopped back on the bed, lying on his side watching James as he rooted around in his closet. He let his mind go blank. He needed rest, not just sleep, but to not worry or do anything. He wanted a break from everything, even thinking.

James glanced over his shoulder, studying Sebastian. "Ready for bed?"

Sebastian scrunched his nose. "No, I'm just trying to turn my brain off."

James smiled, and it was positively evil. "I might have an idea to help with that."

"Oh?" Sebastian sat up, intrigued.

"Come here."

Sebastian was at his side in an instant.

"I've got something I thought you might like to wear."

"In a sexy, fun way?" Sebastian hoped.

"Yeah." James pulled Sebastian's shirt over his head and tossed it aside. "Remember when you said we could role-play losing our virginities to each other."

Excitement built low in Sebastian's belly. "How could I forget?"

James snorted. "Right. Well, I've got a counteroffer for you. Instead of that, because I don't think I need your virginity for you to be mine, how about this...?" He reached into the closet.

Sebastian hung on James's every word. He loved this. Affection overtook his excitement as James extracted a familiar, brightly colored jacket from the closet.

"Put it on." James handed Sebastian his old letterman jacket. "We might not have figured it out back then, but we belonged to each other, even when we weren't together. Even when we didn't speak or do more than stare from afar. You should have been walking around school in this, so let's make up for lost time."

Sebastian pulled the jacket on, grinning. It fit about as well as James's leather jacket, though this one was slightly smaller in the shoulders.

James gazed at him tenderly. He ran a hand up Sebastian's arm, caressing the fabric. "Come see how you look."

Sebastian followed James into the bathroom. He looked funny in the ill-fitting jacket without a shirt, but James's expression said he thought otherwise.

He crowded Sebastian up against the counter, pressing into Sebastian's back, and nuzzled his neck, sending tingles up and down Sebastian's spine. "Perfect."

Sebastian leaned against James. "I like thinking I was always yours." It warmed him to imagine that even when he'd felt alone, he'd belonged to someone.

"Me too." James ran his hand under the jacket, around Sebastian's waist, and down to the front of his jeans.

Sebastian's breath hitched as James popped the button and slid the zipper down.

He pulled down Sebastian's pants, followed by his underwear. "I'm not so interested in pretending we're young again and doing this for the first time. I'm interested in being with you now and rewriting your past so you know someone was always waiting to love you."

"James," Sebastian gasped as his heart all but burst with tenderness. He gripped the counter, steadying himself, and their eyes met in the mirror.

"I've got you." James caressed Sebastian's bare skin, his gaze full of deep affection as he kissed Sebastian's neck. He had to know how much this meant. What a gift his words were.

After such a draining day, Sebastian needed this. James knew just how to take care of him.

"Bend forward for me?" he murmured in Sebastian's ear.

Sebastian braced himself and stuck his ass out. He'd do anything to have this. To feel claimed and loved.

James cupped Sebastian's fully exposed rear, then reached into a drawer, barely breaking eye contact in the mirror as he did so. He found lube and squeezed some onto his fingers before pressing between Sebastian's ass cheeks, finding his hole.

Sebastian groaned at the contact, spreading his legs wider. He watched James's reflection as James massaged his rim and James watched him back, their eyes locked.

Something about the mirror intensified the connection. They'd looked into each other's eyes during intimate moments plenty of times but none had felt like this, like they were seeing something new unfold between them.

As James breached Sebastian with a finger, his gaze fell, watching Sebastian take him. Sebastian took in the scene reflected before him, becoming more aware of his own body as he caught his own reactions in the mirror, the way his cheeks flushed and chest heaved.

Their eyes met again, and James's cheeks darkened. He worked Sebastian open, getting him ready with efficient, practiced motions, giving Sebastian what he needed without making him wait.

"Now," Sebastian breathed.

James pulled his fingers out, tore off his shirt, and shoved his jeans and underwear out of the way. He slicked himself and pressed against Sebastian's hole.

"I love you," he said, gaze locked on Sebastian in the mirror.

"I love you too." Sebastian arched his back, unable to miss how desperate he looked, blushing all the way down to his neck, mouth parted as he waited eagerly to be filled.

James didn't break his stare as he pushed in. Sebastian accepted him with a moan, getting everything the lonely boy with a hopeless crush that still lived inside him needed.

Sebastian may never have worn the letterman jacket back when he was that boy, but it didn't matter. James was right. They hadn't figured out what to do with their feelings for each other or been each other's firsts when they were young, but that didn't mean the two of them weren't always meant to be. Sebastian could look back, knowing good things were coming. He could look at his past, knowing James was meant for him and that his loneliness was destined to be temporary.

James gripped Sebastian's hips and thrust, starting slow and firm, making Sebastian crave more. Sebastian was hot with lust, skin tingling and cock aching. A knowing look passed between them, and James began fucking Sebastian at the hard pace he lived for, James's muscles tensing and flexing as he pounded into Sebastian, his face displaying his utter devotion.

"I love you, Sebastian. You've always been mine."

"Yes," he answered, thrusting back into James as the reality of James's words sunk into his soul.

"Look how beautiful you are." James gripped Sebastian's shoulder with one hand, the other still clutching his hip. "Look how perfectly we fit together."

James's cock slid in and out of Sebastian, dragging along his prostate. Sebastian felt consumed. Watching James fuck him like this was as intense as the physical feelings. Sebastian loved seeing the needy look in his own eyes as well as James's.

Sebastian reached for his dick, unable to resist.

"Wait." James caught his arm. "I promise it'll be worth it."

Sebastian groaned in frustration but put his hand back on the counter. "Okay, I trust you."

James moaned and picked up his pace.

Sebastian wondered if he'd come without needing to touch himself. It felt that good. He couldn't get enough of the way their skin slapped and their heavy breaths filled the small room.

"Fill me, James. Claim me," Sebastian begged.

James's gaze raked over their reflections, settling on Sebastian's face. He gripped Sebastian's hair, tilting his head back, and thrust once, twice, then stiffened as he came.

Sebastian whimpered. He was so keyed up, so ready to come, and James filling him only made him more desperate.

James pressed his hips tight against Sebastian's ass, cock twitching inside him. He kept his gaze focused on Sebastian in the mirror like he was trying to memorize him.

"Please, James," Sebastian moaned. He ached to touch himself. James had never denied him before.

"You feel so good, sweetheart." James let the hand in Sebastian's hair trail down his neck in a gentle caress, taking a moment to catch his breath. His eyes dropped to where they were joined, and he watched himself pull out.

Sebastian whined at the loss. Before he could start begging again, James pulled him up and spun him around.

James sank to his knees, Sebastian's neglected cock level with his mouth. "Spread your legs wider."

Sebastian adjusted his stance. James ran his hands up Sebastian's thighs. He tugged on Sebastian's balls as his other hand slipped between Sebastian's cheeks and filled him with three fingers.

"*Uh.*" Sebastian gripped James's head as his knees went weak.

"I can feel my cum inside you." James pushed his fingers deeper. "Fuck, sweetheart."

"Oh my god, James." Sebastian trembled, cum running down his inner thighs.

James sucked Sebastian's cock into his mouth, swirling his tongue. He bobbed his head and thrust his fingers. James had been right. This was worth the wait, but Sebastian was too close to last long. It was all too good. He let out a cry as James found his prostate and started to come.

With James's name on his lips, Sebastian thrust through his orgasm, lost in the heat of James's mouth. James swallowed, looking up as he worked his fingers, sending Sebastian higher.

Sebastian had never seen so much love in someone's eyes, and it was all for him.

12

JAMES

The sinkhole was definitely getting bigger.

James stood at the edge of the clearing with Sebastian the next morning, eyeing it. "It has to be twice the size it was before." James was glad he'd thought to move the fuel cell last time. It might have fallen in otherwise.

Sebastian took a hesitant step forward. "Should we look in? Maybe we can see better than Eli could since it's bigger now."

James reluctantly agreed. The rope was still tied to the tree, and after checking the knot was secure, he had Sebastian tie the other end around his waist.

Sebastian gave him slack as he inched forward. The ground felt solid, but he didn't let that stop him from walking like he was on thin ice.

"It still feels pretty stable," he called back to Sebastian when he was a foot from the edge. "It's a sheer break. Doesn't look like the soil is slowly crumbling in."

"Sounds unnatural," Sebastian replied. "But we knew this had to be magical."

James couldn't see much in the hole. It seemed unusually dark. Satisfied the ground wouldn't fall away, he lay on his

89

stomach and inched forward until he could peer over the edge. "There's nothing to see. It's completely dark."

"What if you send a light down?"

That was a good idea. James summoned a small ball of light and let it descend into the hole. It was only about four feet across, but the light didn't fill the space as it should. It was like its rays weren't leaving the ball, illuminating nothing around it.

James urged the light farther down. It got smaller as it went, showing him nothing but how deep the hole actually was. Then it disappeared.

"It's gone." James stared downward in case he missed the light popping back up. There wasn't even a flicker. James couldn't feel the spell anymore and didn't think it was taking any more of his energy. It was like the light had gone out or the spell had failed, but it didn't feel the same as when his concentration broke and he lost a spell that way.

"Think you just sent light to Beyond?" Sebastian asked.

It was a freaky thought. "Maybe." He scooted back and stood. "I wonder if the spell can continue working once it's left this world. It doesn't feel like it is."

James returned to Sebastian, who untied the rope.

"Do you think this makes it easier for things to pass through the gateway?" Sebastian glanced over James's shoulder at the hole as he spoke. He sucked in a breath and grabbed James's arm, grip crushing and eyes wide.

"What?" James asked in alarm, whipping around to look. He didn't see anything.

"I swear a shadowy hand was gripping the edge, right where you just were."

The clearing was mostly free of shadow and bright sunlight covered the ground where James had been lying. He didn't see anything else.

James turned back to Sebastian to find fear written all over his face. Sweat broke out on James's forehead. "It's daylight. Surely shades can't come through now."

Sebastian remained fixated on the hole. "Probably not, luckily for us. That must be why it retreated, or maybe it was banished by the sun."

It was a marginally comforting thought. The shade must have seen James's orb of light and come to investigate. Meaning that creatures in Beyond knew they were here, poking around on the other side of the gateway. A chill ran down James's spine.

Something else occurred to James. "Wouldn't the sun have banished the shade before it got to the edge of the hole?"

Sebastian hummed in thought. "Maybe, but whatever is in the hole seems to be keeping light out. Otherwise, we'd be able to see inside, so maybe not."

James liked that logic. It meant the shade Sebastian thought he saw was less likely to be fully sunlight resistant. Completely light-resistant shades were the last thing they needed.

Still, James and Sebastian watched the hole for a long, tense moment, waiting. Nothing happened, which hopefully meant the shade had been banished and hadn't just retreated, but James didn't find much comfort in the uncertainty they were left with.

Sebastian threw the rope down at the base of the tree. "There's not much more we can do here. Let's get Eli's data and go."

They made quick work of gathering the receipts and left the property. James drove them back to Gray Electrical, the ride quiet other than the music Sebastian selected. When they pulled up at the shop, Hazel was outside helping someone fill their car battery.

The customer seemed to stop chatting with Hazel as soon as they caught sight of Sebastian. James pursed his lips as he passed them on his way inside.

He could kill William for turning people against Sebastian, never mind trapping them unnecessarily and putting their lives at risk. James was sure that if most of the people in the auditorium yesterday had heard about the veins from Eleanor instead of William, there wouldn't be anywhere near as much animosity toward Sebastian.

To his credit, Sebastian seemed to be handling it well. It just wasn't fair. James wanted to protect Sebastian from the pain of any more rejection. He knew he couldn't. He just wished the world were kinder. He wished he and Sebastian didn't have to fight so hard to get to the happy, simple life they wanted.

"Want some coffee?" he asked Sebastian once they were inside.

Sebastian flashed a sweet smile, dimples framing his face. "Sure."

James went to make it, hoping Sebastian hadn't noticed the customer's reaction outside.

Hazel joined them a minute later. "Do I want to know how Storm House was this morning?"

"No," James said before recounting everything for her anyway. "The fuel cell has dropped more too. Another big dip in energy."

"Wonder if the bigger dips coincide with the hole growing," Hazel said as she lined mugs up on the counter for James to fill. "Oh, guess what? Eleanor told me William wasn't at work this morning, no explanation given for his absence."

James grunted, his hate for the man clear. No words needed.

"We know he can't have gone far," Sebastian said with grim amusement.

Hazel laughed. "No, he'll be lurking. Just figures he'd be all confident pointing his finger at you yesterday and then not show his face around town hall now that he knows not everyone agrees with him."

"They don't?" Sebastian asked, sounding surprised.

James's heart pinched. "Of course they don't."

"Not at all," Hazel agreed. "Especially after they were told the truth. Eleanor is way more respected than William. It's one of the reasons she's mayor. People listen to her. Seeing her support you changed people's minds. The meeting was tense, but that wasn't the end of it."

The shop bell rang, and all three of them turned. There, standing on the retail side of the room, was William himself.

"Speak of the fucking devil," Hazel muttered. "Hi," she called loud enough for him to hear, making her way over. "Is there something you need?"

William narrowed his eyes at Hazel, probably picking up on her less-than-friendly tone.

Hazel leaned against the counter, pulling off a casual I-don't-trust-or-like-you stance. William didn't say anything, which wasn't like him. James had never known the man to keep anything to himself.

William turned away from Hazel and scrutinized the store. James was glad he wasn't starting in on Sebastian, but if he wasn't planning to harass him, why was he here? Was his presence some sort of intimidation, like a warning that he was watching them?

"I don't think you have what I need," William said at last.

"Sorry," Hazel replied, not sounding sorry at all.

William glared at her and then turned his narrowed eyes on James and Sebastian. "I'll be seeing you around, unfortunately." He left the shop without a backward glance.

Hazel returned to the work side of the shop and grabbed her mug. "He's certainly using his time ditching work wisely." She rolled her eyes.

James sat at his desk, preparing to type up the data they'd gathered from the clearing since Eli was working at the diner that morning. Sebastian grabbed a spare chair and settled in next to him, reading out the numbers. James found it hard to see the point in recording more of the veins' energy flow. Was any of this information helping them?

Hazel assisted a few more customers at the pumps. By late morning, she and James packed up and left the shop to continue fixing the lights in town, starting with one in front of the post office.

Sebastian, who'd come along with them, got a phone call. James perked up, hoping it was Sebastian's mom, even though he hated that Sebastian had to deal with her. She might have answers, and James was getting desperate enough to hope she'd help.

"It's my lawyer." Sebastian accepted the call and wandered to the grass by the stone to talk. James tried to fend off his disappointment.

"I'm beginning to feel like nothing we're doing is worth the effort," James admitted to Hazel.

She gave him a sympathetic frown. "We can't do nothing."

"I know." James nudged the toolbox sitting on the sidewalk with his foot. "But take the lights, for example. Is replacing them pointless? They'll probably get smashed out again. And that hand in the clearing today could mean shades resistant to daylight are coming or are already here." He assumed the shade in the clearing had been banished by the daylight, but he couldn't shake the fear it hadn't been.

Hazel shrugged helplessly. "Not fixing the lights feels like giving up. We have to do what we can."

"I know. And I don't want to give up." James was determined not to. "But we don't have control over this situation, and everything we do is a reminder. What if that horrible shade comes back and casts spells on the veins again? What if it makes the imbalance even more unstable?"

"I don't know, James." Hazel gripped his shoulder. It would have been more comforting if there wasn't obvious fear in Hazel's eyes.

Sebastian walked back over to them, his phone call apparently finished.

"Anything?" James asked.

Sebastian grimaced. "Owning part of Nelson Power doesn't

give me access to their intellectual property. Even offering to exchange my shares for the information got me nowhere. Whatever they know isn't getting out. I can't even get more information on Nelson Storm. Being a descendant doesn't seem to mean much."

"Oh well, it's what we expected." James tried his best not to be dejected. The secret of how to safely extract power from the veins was never the most likely solution, so not finding it out wasn't a setback. Still, it would have felt better to be able to try taking power from the veins and see what happened to rule it out completely.

Doing nothing was killing them slowly, but there wasn't anything else to say about the dead end, so James and Hazel got back to fixing the lights while Sebastian sat against a nearby tree and listened to music.

Now that the darkness was gone, all the tourists seemed to have returned. People were in and out of Beth's souvenir shop, wandering around the circle and taking pictures of the stone.

For the first time, the peaceful familiarity of Moonlight Falls didn't comfort James. Seeing things go on as if nothing was wrong put him on edge.

James couldn't help scrutinizing all the locals who passed by. Most of them probably hadn't found out about the veins, but he was wary of anyone who'd been at the meeting. He noticed a woman standing by the ice cream shop who seemed to be staring at them. He frowned at her. She wasn't familiar, so it was unlikely she was a Moonlighter or had been at the meeting, but James swore she was looking at Sebastian.

Sebastian had his eyes closed. He looked dazzling sitting under the tree, surrounded by fall leaves, soft autumn light warming his skin. The season suited him, the fall colors complementing his ginger hair and rosy cheeks. James suspected spring and summer would suit him just as well. He'd look absolutely ethereal, surrounded by all the freshly blooming flowers, and would enjoy the long days spent in his garden.

James couldn't wait to see the seasons change with Sebastian. He longed for the years ahead and all the little routines they would build together.

Sebastian opened his eyes and looked at James from beneath his lashes. A deeper red tinged Sebastian's cheeks in response to whatever expression he found on James's face. Fuck, James loved him so much.

The back of James's neck prickled, and his attention was torn from Sebastian. He looked across the street to find the woman still staring. James glanced between her and Sebastian, not sure what had her attention.

Sebastian followed his gaze. He sat up abruptly, all the softness leaving his features. Sebastian slowly pulled the headphones off his ears.

"What's wrong?" James asked.

Sebastian didn't speak right away, and when he did, his voice was barely audible. "That's my mom."

13

SEBASTIAN

Sebastian was stunned. It was more likely he'd fallen asleep under the tree and this was a dream or nightmare than his mom had actually shown up. He'd never imagined he'd see her again.

But there Samantha Storm stood. Was she going to come over or just gawk from afar? Sebastian certainly wasn't going to her.

"That's your mom?" James asked in disbelief, stepping partially in front of Sebastian as if trying to shield him.

"The one and only," Sebastian said dryly.

Hazel came up beside them. "She better be here to help."

James snorted. "Don't count on it."

Now that three people were staring at her, Samantha seemed to decide it was time to approach. Sebastian didn't get off the ground. He wasn't sure if he could. He'd been half-ready to face his mom over the phone but after her not answering repeatedly, he'd begun to worry he'd never hear from her again.

He hadn't been prepared for this.

His mom walked toward him like she was trying to act casual, her face carefully neutral. However, the death grip on her handbag gave away her nerves. She didn't acknowledge James or

Hazel as she looked down at Sebastian sitting in the dirt. "Sebastian."

What a greeting. Totally worthy of twelve years apart.

Sebastian stood. He was a full head taller than his mother now. He turned to James. "You might want to check if hell froze over."

James blinked at him, his grumpy expression cracking to show a hint of amusement.

Sebastian turned back to his mom. "Or maybe the world really is ending. I can't think why else you'd be here."

She took a breath like she was trying to calm herself. "Now's not the time for jokes, Sebastian."

"It's always the time for jokes," he insisted like the contrary child he'd always been.

His mom sighed, making a show of her exhaustion. She looked old. Then again, Sebastian supposed he did too, compared to the last time they'd been face to face. Samantha had always dyed her hair a dark auburn, so she didn't show her age through any grays. But she had more lines around her face and something about the way she was dressed didn't match with what Sebastian remembered.

There was a very long, awkward moment where no one spoke. Hazel turned away and went back to work. Sebastian didn't blame her. He wouldn't mind avoiding this too.

"I take it you're here to talk about the veins?" Sebastian asked.

His mom gasped, looking frantically between him and James. Right. She didn't know anyone else knew the family secret.

"He knows. It's fine." Sebastian waved a careless hand. "He saved me from Storm House, actually. Mom, meet James Gray, my boyfriend."

"James…Gray?" she muttered more to herself than anyone. "Boyfriend?"

Sebastian cocked his head. "Yeah. You knew I was bi, right? Or maybe not. I never came out to you."

Samantha's expression turned scolding. "I don't care that you're bi. I care that he *knows*. What do you mean he saved you? What did you do, Sebastian?"

"What did *he* do?" James took a step forward. "What about what you did?"

Sebastian expected his mom to deny she'd done anything. Instead, she took a nervous step backward, giving Sebastian a guilty look.

She adjusted her grip on her handbag. "There's a lot to discuss. Why don't we go somewhere less public?"

Sebastian looped his arm through James's. "My house is right around the corner."

He led them to the duplex, James saying a hasty goodbye to Hazel, who offered a sympathetic frown.

Sebastian unlocked the front door and ushered his mom inside. She seemed shell-shocked, looking around the bare living room like she'd never seen the inside of a house before.

Her eyes landed on the box of old papers on the table. "This is from Storm House."

"Yep." Sebastian sat beside the box, James at his side.

His mom sat opposite them. "How are you here?" she asked, tone imploring.

Sebastian ignored her. He wasn't handing out information for free. "How's Kira?"

Samantha's hands tightened on her handbag. "Good. Far away from here."

"Oh well, as long as she's safe."

Samantha closed her eyes. "Sebastian, please."

"Please, what? Pretend you didn't sacrifice me for her? I know you were never planning on having to own up to it since I only found out what you'd been doing all my life once I was trapped and unable to reach you."

"You're right. I never wanted to face this. How could I? How could I ever look at you again after what I did?"

Sebastian swallowed a lump in his throat. "You're looking at me now."

"Yes." She set her bag aside and folded her hands in front of her.

"Why didn't you answer my letters?" Sebastian choked on the words. Fuck, this hurt. He hadn't planned to ask that. It just came out. He didn't want to relive her rejection, but now that he was sitting across from his mother, he had to know.

"I couldn't face my own guilt." Samantha made a pained sound, looking away from him. "You have to understand. I didn't do this because I wanted to. What would you have done if you found out your child was damned to live a cursed life?"

"Not curse another child, that's for sure," James cut in, stern and unforgiving.

Samantha fixed a hollow gaze on James. "I know it wasn't right, but I couldn't see past protecting my kid."

"And I wasn't your kid?"

Samantha looked at the table.

"Fine, don't answer." Sebastian sat up straighter. "You've already made it perfectly clear you didn't want me. Whatever, it's in the past. But it doesn't explain why you ignored me after the deed was done and I was trapped. Why not tell me where you last saw Selma's spell? Why not help me at all? You knew I was alone. For years."

A tear fell down Samantha's cheek, but Sebastian refused to care. "What I did was horrible. I know. I couldn't live with the reality of it after Stephen died. I was sorry I did what I did, but there was no taking it back."

"But you made it worse," James said. "You could have visited Sebastian. Helped him. You could have changed his imprison-ment and made it bearable. Hell, you could have done that for your brother like your mother did for your father. You didn't have to abandon either of them."

"I know," Samantha pleaded, even as she glared at James for voicing truths she clearly didn't like looking at. "I did the wrong thing at every turn. But the only way I could act like it was worth it was if I forgot about Storm House."

"You're selfish," Sebastian said.

"I am." She nodded grimly like this was something she had no control over but accepted. "I chose my own comfort and my daughter's life over everything else. You're entitled to hate me for it."

Sebastian rubbed his eyes, the beginning of a headache pulsing uncomfortably. "That doesn't actually make me feel any better."

"Well, what do you want me to do about it? I'll never make it up to you. I'll never put this right. Not after nearly three decades of choosing to let others suffer so my daughter and I didn't have to."

There was a heavy pause. Sebastian didn't know what to say. The past couldn't be changed. It would always hurt.

James took Sebastian's hand, lacing their fingers together and stroking his thumb lightly over Sebastian's skin. "You can't make things up to Sebastian, but you owe him everything you know about the curse and the veins. You may have come here to find out what was going on to see if the curse would come for your daughter, but you can choose to help. For once."

"You seem to have a lot of opinions on something that has nothing to do with you," Samantha snapped.

"Nothing to do with me?" James's voice turned cold. He ran his free hand through his hair, his gaze cutting to Sebastian. He seemed to reconsider his next words. "We can get to *that* later. We're not telling you anything until you share everything you know."

Samantha eyed Sebastian like she wasn't taking James's word for anything.

Sebastian tried to ignore the growing ache in his head. Fuck he was tired. Of this and everything he had to deal with. "If you want to find out what's happening with the curse, it's the only way."

"I don't see how telling you about the veins will help." Frustration leaked into Samantha's tone. "Who's out at Storm House now? I assume you found Selma's spell and trapped someone."

"Not all of us will damn innocent people to save ourselves, Mom. You don't need to understand how talking to me will help. You just have to do it. Or would you rather keep secrets on the off chance that revealing them will hurt you and Kira? Are you going to make the same choice you supposedly regret? Or will you do the right thing this time?"

After a long pause, she said, "What do you want to know exactly? I assume Stephen told you everything."

"Why don't we compare notes and check? He might have missed some things, seeing as he was dying." Sebastian had a lot of anger for Stephen after he died, but he'd loved his uncle too. His mom's flinch at the blunt reminder of Stephen's death gave him a stab of guilt for using it as a weapon. He shook it off. "Tell me everything your dad told you about how the imbalance started and what his father and Nelson did."

Samantha ran a hand through her hair. "He was only little when it all happened and didn't tell Stephen or me anything until he was dying. I don't know—"

"Mom, please."

She gave Sebastian a barely-there nod. "Okay. Apparently, Sullivan and Selma weren't as secretive about things as my father was when Stephen and I were growing up. We didn't know about the curse, but everyone in the generations before us did. The whole family knew the secret back then. My father knew what was coming for him well ahead of time. My mother knew too. But they decided not to tell my brother and me. We weren't there for the initial disaster, so we might not understand

and therefore try to escape our duty, or so their justification went."

"And learning the secret never trapped anyone?" Sebastian asked.

Samantha gave him a confused look. "No. Selma told who she wanted, and they were prevented from telling anyone else by the secret-binding. She died not long after my father and mother were married." She turned to James, her gaze sharpening. "How did you find out? Did you break the secret-binding and get trapped?"

James didn't respond.

"Right. You two aren't telling me anything." Samantha turned back to Sebastian. "Sullivan and Nelson were scientists. They bought the property to study the veins. Nelson was always confident veins could be used as an energy source. He wanted to power the house with them as some sort of experiment. The brothers filled my father's young mind with all their ideas, and even decades later, he spoke highly of their intellect."

Sebastian leaned forward, feeling like the explanation he needed was just out of reach. "If they were scientists, why was there no information on the veins at Storm House? Wouldn't they have kept records? I never found anything technical."

"Nelson took a lot of it when he left. The rest Sullivan burned, according to my father." Samantha shrugged as if the burned records didn't matter. "Sullivan—my grandfather—was never secret-bound, so he could have told my brother and me everything just as Selma had done before him, but when Dad decided we shouldn't know in case we tried to escape our duty, Grandpa Sullivan got rid of anything that might hint at the problem so there would be no stumbling across the truth."

"What were they doing to the veins when they created the imbalance?" Sebastian fixed his mom with a hard stare. "Was it an experiment trying to extract power? Did they take energy out?"

Samantha looked surprised. "It was an experiment, yes. Dad

said he'd been excited and wanted to watch, but they wouldn't let him. He was only six."

Sebastian didn't really care about the young Simon Storm right now. "What did they do?"

"They didn't take energy," Samantha said. "They weren't able to harness the raw power at all. They took a piece of the vein itself."

14

SEBASTIAN

"A PIECE OF THE VEIN?" Sebastian shot a confused look at James, who seemed just as surprised. "Like a physical piece?"

"That's what Dad said."

Sebastian shook his head. This couldn't be right. "How is that possible? A vein is a fluid system, like a river. You can take energy out like you can take water, but you can't take a piece like it's a pie."

Samantha raised her hands, as if to say *what do you want from me*. "I'm just telling you what Dad told me. A piece of the vein. They thought it could be used as an energy source. Instead, it broke the natural order of the system, causing the energy at the intersection to go haywire. I don't know the scientific details, but the veins couldn't maintain themselves without the missing piece."

"What happened to the piece?" James asked.

"It got destroyed," Samantha said to Sebastian's dismay. "As soon as they extracted it, it began to deteriorate."

"So we can't put it back?" Sebastian asked desperately.

"There's nothing left of it. It's been gone for eighty years." Samantha narrowed her eyes. "Why does it matter?"

"Because if we don't fix the veins, they're going to blow." Sebastian fisted his hands in his hair, pulling hard. *Fuck.*

"So get the hell out of here, Sebastian," his mom said as if he was being obtuse.

"We can't get out of here," Sebastian growled. James placed a comforting hand on his back. "I'm not trapped at Storm House, but I'm still stuck. And it's not just me."

Samantha's eyes widened. "If you're still tied to the veins, why are they at risk of exploding?"

Sebastian didn't feel like explaining. "There has to be a way to solve this. We have to be able to restore the veins."

"Selma did," his mom reminded him. "She created a stand-in for the missing piece."

Sebastian turned desperately to James, only to see his own fear reflected on his face. This problem had no better solution. What had been broken couldn't be put back together. The key to it all had been destroyed the moment this problem had begun.

They were doomed.

"Sebastian, what exactly is going on?" his mother's words cut through his panic.

He turned back to her. "Moonlight Falls has a lot more problems than potential explosion. Did you know the vein intersection is a gateway?"

"*What?*" She looked genuinely shocked. "To Beyond?"

"Fuck." None of this was helping. Sebastian kicked the table leg, not bothering to answer her.

James remained calm. He seemed to be studying Samantha. "What do you mean Selma created a stand-in for the missing piece?"

"How can I be clearer than that?" She frowned at James in pure annoyance. "The person trapped by the curse does what the missing piece can't. The person makes the system whole by supplying energy and allowing the veins' energy to pass through them."

"But if a stand-in is no longer enough, what do we do?" Sebastian asked.

"I don't know." Samantha stood from the table. "I'm sorry, Sebastian. I've told you what you asked for."

Sebastian stood, his chair legs scraping the floor. "Are you leaving?" He hated the desperate edge to his voice. Even after everything, he didn't want his mom to walk away from him. He didn't particularly want her around, but he couldn't stand being abandoned again.

"Is there any point in me staying?" She picked up her handbag. "If things are falling apart and on their way to exploding, there's no reason for me to stay."

"No." Sebastian felt hollow inside. "Why stand by your son? Why choose me? What would that be worth?"

Samantha scowled at him, her eyes angry. "There's no sense in me staying to die. Or would that make you happy?"

Sebastian felt like he'd been slapped. "Of course not. That wasn't… Never mind."

James rose from the table, rounding it to approach Samantha. "You could try to help us find a solution."

"What solution? The missing piece is gone. Selma did her best to replace it through blood and bone, but if that's not working, I don't know what you expect me to do." She marched to the front door and threw it open, leaving without another glance in Sebastian's direction.

James's face twisted in a way Sebastian had never seen before, like he was about to explode. "She can't just walk away."

Sebastian wished he could pretend it didn't hurt. He knew

better than to expect anything different from his mother, but somehow, she still got to him. At least he'd probably never have to see her again.

James turned away from the open front door and engulfed Sebastian in a hug. "I'm sorry, sweetheart."

"You don't have to be." Sebastian pressed his face into James's hair. "This sucks, but I've got you. Your support means everything."

"I wish I could do more," James whispered.

"This is enough, James."

James held him for a long time. Sebastian wondered if James felt just as lost about what to do next as he did.

Eventually, they returned to town and found Hazel. Their grim expressions must have alerted her to the bad news because she didn't immediately ask how things went.

"Let's find Parker and Eli," James suggested.

Eli was due to finish his shift at the diner, and when they arrived, it looked like Parker was too. They all settled in the park at a picnic table near the trees. All they needed was some possessed deer or a bear to come crash the party and the day would be a perfect shitshow. Though Sebastian was too consumed by everything his mother had said to spare any real concern for shades.

Sebastian explained what they'd learned. Eli looked like his mind was being blown when he heard a piece of the vein had been taken. Sebastian marveled at the younger man's unwavering intellectual interest.

"It'd be fascinating to know how they did it," Eli mused. "I doubt anyone else has ever taken a piece of a vein."

"Unless they did and blew up because of it," Parker countered.

Eli frowned. "True. Sorry, this is just fascinating. Academically, I mean."

"If only it meant we weren't screwed," Sebastian said, half in the hope someone would tell him they weren't.

"Maybe we need to redo Selma's spell," Eli suggested. "We could try to recreate it, rebind an energy source to the veins and get back to the stability she had originally."

Sebastian didn't think any of them were capable of that kind of magic. Parker was powerful, but he didn't seem to do much bespoke spellwork beyond warding. Creating spells was a challenge, especially blood-and-bone spells, which none of them had any real knowledge of.

As Sebastian opened his mouth to say all this, something rushed out of the woods. A shade left the shadows of the trees and flew toward them, circling before diving downward, aiming for Eli.

Eli threw up his hands instinctually. James and Parker both sent sparks flying. To Sebastian's surprise, the shade didn't grab Eli. The sparks missed as it dove past him and grabbed his backpack, which had been discarded on the ground.

"Hey! What?" Eli twisted around in confusion.

Sebastian and James leaped from the picnic table. The shade shot into the sky in full sunlight. It clutched Eli's backpack and leered down at them.

Sebastian, James, Hazel, and Parker shot sparks in the air, but the shade flew higher to avoid them. It was nothing like the humanoid shade but still looked different from a typical one. It wasn't made of ghostly semi-transparent shadow but a dark black substance that seemed to eat the light. Otherwise, its body and bony arms were a familiar ghostly shape.

The shade shot back toward the forest, flying above the trees and disappearing from view.

"Why would it steal your backpack?" Sebastian asked, thinking bitterly of his stolen robe.

"I don't know." Eli stared into the trees. "I guess there wasn't anything else for it to grab."

But why grab anything?

Parker put a hand on Eli's shoulder. "Did you lose any of your research?"

Eli shook his head. "No, everything in my bag I'd already copied, though it's never good to lose the primary data source. I had a bunch of old receipts in there. At least my laptop is at home."

Hazel glared at the forest. "That shade out on a bright day isn't good."

Eli jolted like he hadn't even thought of that, too focused on his stolen bag.

Sebastian tried to find a positive. "At least it didn't stick around."

"It seemed like it came just to take my bag," Eli said. "Like it was planned."

James looked at his brother with concern. "Do you think it could have known you were carrying research on the veins? Remember how the shades tried to grab your backpack at Storm House when all those shades were surrounding the fuel cell?"

Sebastian sat back down at the picnic table. The surprise shade hadn't helped his headache. "How could it have known Eli was carrying his research? There definitely weren't any shades like *that* in the clearing that day."

"But they've clearly realized I'm doing something with the veins and must be able to communicate with each other." Eli bit his lip. "Shades have been messing with my experiments from the start. What if they don't want me doing anything with the veins because they don't want me messing with their gateway?"

Parker seemed to go pale as something occurred to him. "Maybe you *were* targeted all those weeks ago and the bite you suffered wasn't random."

No one seemed happy about that revelation, but Eli rallied quickly. "Stealing my stuff won't stop me, and they won't learn much from what was in my bag," he said with vindictive satisfaction.

"Who knows, if they're so concerned with their gateway, maybe the shades will realize the veins are getting less stable and fix them for us," Sebastian joked.

James snorted. "Wouldn't that be nice?"

It felt just about as unlikely as any other solution.

15

JAMES

JAMES INSISTED they stay at the duplex that night. He wanted to keep an eye on the town and see if there was more shade activity. After confirming there were indeed shades resistant enough to light to be unhindered by direct sunlight, James couldn't escape the feeling that something big was brewing. Maybe another wave of darkness was coming or something else they couldn't yet fathom.

Watching for shades also gave James a sense of purpose. Learning there was no restoring the veins, other than by a work-around similar to Selma's, left him lost.

He wasn't sure what to make of the sun-resistant shade either. If some of the beasts could be out during the day, why hadn't they seen more of them? Why had there been a herd of possessed deer? Were the stronger shades hiding to try and keep people from realizing some of them could withstand full sunlight, waiting to launch a surprise daytime attack, or was the one they'd seen a lone daylight-resistant one?

Sebastian leaned against James as they sat on the bed, looking out the window. He'd been quiet since seeing his mom. Part of James wished he'd given the woman more of a piece of his mind, but it was probably best he hadn't. Sebastian knew where James stood, and Sebastian's relationship with Samantha was for him to work out. James's job was to support Sebastian and remind him he had trustworthy people in his life who would stand by him and treat him right, not get caught up in his own dislike for the woman.

They hadn't seen many shades so far. A few hovered around the street but didn't seem to be doing anything.

James rubbed Sebastian's thigh. "You should get some rest."

"I had a nap this afternoon," he reminded James, even though James hadn't forgotten. "Besides, my head is feeling better."

"Okay, good." James turned back to the window, arm around Sebastian. "We can't stay up all night though."

"We could do shifts. But even if we see anything, there's no guarantee we can do something about it."

"At least Parker warded the stone." James stared at the rock, hoping the protective spell would stop the shades from doing the dance that had brought on the darkness.

Eli hadn't had a chance to test if the stone had any magic, and there was no warding the veins. Who knew, even without the stone, shades might be able to work their spells on Moonlight Falls when their leader returned.

The few shades in the center of town didn't seem interested in the stone. One darted swiftly across the circle from the diner toward town hall, completely ignoring it. As James watched the shade, he noticed a figure standing on the sidewalk shrouded in shadow because the light in front of town hall hadn't been fixed yet.

James stood from the bed. "Look." He approached the window, followed by Sebastian.

"It's a person," Sebastian said in disbelief.

The shade simply hovered in front of the person for a few moments, then darted back the way it'd come. At first, James wondered if the figure might have been the humanoid shade, but it definitely wasn't. The person didn't seem very tall and moved much more normally than the otherworldly being had. At least the shade had left the person alone.

James and Sebastian watched as the person headed in their direction. As the figure passed under a streetlight, James let out a grunt of annoyance. "It's William."

"What the hell is he doing in town at night?"

"Nothing good."

"That's a given." Sebastian snorted a dry laugh.

William continued down the sidewalk until he was out of sight. Maybe he'd been at town hall late to avoid people after ditching work and was parked around the corner. James turned his attention back to the shades. A few were peering in the closed diner windows, not unlike what they'd often done at Storm House.

Around eleven, James was too tired to keep watching. The shades had disappeared and nothing seemed to be happening. He and Sebastian settled into bed, Sebastian falling asleep almost instantly. James eventually drifted off too.

He jerked awake suddenly, not knowing how long it had been. He swore he'd heard a noise. James strained his ears, and there it was again, followed by a sound like a door closing.

James sat bolt upright. Was someone or something in the duplex?

"Sebastian." He gently shook his shoulder. "Wake up."

"Hm?" Sebastian blinked at him in the dark.

"Something's in the house."

Sebastian sat up in alarm. Simultaneously, they slid out of bed. Sebastian gabbed a hoodie to put on over his boxer briefs, but James didn't bother.

There was a creak downstairs.

"A shade wouldn't make any noise," Sebastian whispered. "And the duplex is warded."

Then what the hell was it? Had their protections been broken while they'd slept?

The bedroom door stood open. James moved through it quickly and as quietly as he could. At the top of the stairs, he peered down but couldn't see anything in the stairwell.

James pointed down the stairs, indicating he was going to check the ground floor. Sebastian nodded, following close behind. Luckily, the stairs and bedroom were carpeted, muffling their steps. James heard another creak from the room below. He held a wind spell in the back of his mind, ready to use it and strike out at anything they came across to knock it back.

He was two steps from the bottom when a figure appeared in front of him. William. The man froze in the dark like he was startled to see James and Sebastian standing there.

"What the hell?" Sebastian shouted.

James abandoned wind for light. His spell flared, and William squinted dramatically.

"Hey," he grunted, covering his face as if having a light shone in it was unreasonable.

"*Hey*? You're in my house," Sebastian growled.

William backed up a step, and James and Sebastian pushed forward. As they exited the stairway, the rest of the living room came into view, revealing three other men. One lunged for the front door and threw it open.

"Stop!" Sebastian shouted, but the guy was gone.

"I've seen the rest of you," James warned. "No point running."

William turned toward the other men. "Come on. Honest mistake. We thought the place was unoccupied. No idea it had been rented out."

"Yeah right." Sebastian switched on the living room light, and James let his spell snuff out. "You broke in. Why bother if you thought no one lived here?"

"What were you doing, William?" James demanded when no one spoke up.

Before William could reply, one of the men—someone James could have sworn was relatively new in town—lunged for James, grabbing him and pinning his arms to his sides.

"Get the other one," the attacker shouted.

The other man—who James would have bet was named Jim Mills—grabbed at Sebastian. James stomped on the insole of the man holding him. He grunted in pain, his hold loosening enough for James to elbow him in the gut and twist free. James grabbed the man going for Sebastian by the back of his shirt.

"Stop now, or I'll be using magic next," James growled.

Both men stood stalk still.

"Where did William go?" Sebastian asked.

"Shit." James looked around. William was nowhere to be seen. "He couldn't have gone far."

"No, all because of you," the man who'd attacked James said, pointing at Sebastian. "You trapped us!"

"Is that why you're here?" James looked between them.

Jim glared. "He needs to go back to Storm House and release us from his curse."

"So you were going to abduct him and try to trap him there?"

"Someone's got to do something." Jim crossed his arms indignantly.

James couldn't believe it. He was almost blind with anger. "And you thought this was justifiable?"

Jim clapped the other man on the shoulder. "Let's go." He gestured to the open door.

James stepped in front of them. "I don't think so. I'm calling the police."

"Got your phone in your underwear," the other man sneered.

Shit, their phones were upstairs.

"We can't go to jail anyway," the man said. "We're trapped, so no one's taking us down to Apple Valley, are they?" They pushed past James to leave.

Sebastian took an unsteady step after them.

James grabbed his arm. "Let them go. They can't escape Moonlight Falls. I'm sure Eleanor will figure out what to do with them. People can't just commit crimes because they're trapped here and unable to be taken to jail."

Sebastian closed the front door. "True." The tension disappeared from his body, leaving him looking scared and hurt.

James wrapped his arms around him. "Are you okay? I mean, of course, you aren't. William just led a group of people to break in and kidnap you."

"Definitely doesn't make me like the duplex any more than before." Sebastian glanced hopelessly around the sparse room. "How did William know I lived here?"

"He must have seen us coming in or out." The only time James had noticed William was when he and Sebastian had been on the way to the duplex, but William had gone into town hall before he could have seen where they were going. He must have seen them another time or seen Sebastian coming and going without James.

James retrieved his phone and called Eleanor, waking the poor woman up. James had never heard her so mad. She said William was dismissed from his position as a city councilor. Sharing the Storm House secret should have been enough to get rid of him, but breaking and entering and attempted kidnapping was a whole other story.

"Let's call the police anyway," Eleanor said. "They can come arrest everyone involved, and when they can't get out of Moonlight Falls with them, at least someone on the outside will know there's something strange going on."

James hung up the phone and rubbed his temple. How could someone violate Sebastian's home like this, and how had they planned to keep him at Storm House? A horrible vision of Sebastian chained up in the musty old manor filled his mind.

"I think I want to live on a hobby farm," Sebastian said out of nowhere.

James stopped rubbing his head. Sebastian was perched on

the couch, curled into his hoodie, looking deeply serious. "What?" James asked.

"I don't know if I want a house in the middle of one of the neighborhoods." Sebastian took a moment to consider this, then nodded in agreement with himself. "I want more space than that and need a field for Miss Moo, not to mention lots of fruit trees and a garden. I just don't want to be as far away as Storm House was or live anywhere that dreary."

James forced his mind to shift gears. "A hobby farm sounds wonderful. Some of the places on the edge of town might work."

Sebastian nodded. "I remember seeing a For Sale sign when we met Eli and Parker by the boundary before the horde of shades attacked."

"We'll check it out," James promised, sitting on the couch next to Sebastian. It sounded perfect and so beautifully normal. Helping Sebastian settle into the life he wanted was what James should be doing, not dealing with veins and mobs of angry Moonlighters.

"I already didn't like this place," Sebastian all but whispered. "Having people break in has completely killed it. I can't believe they were going to attack me and force me back to that house."

"I know, it's horrible. But they won't be getting away with it." James squeezed his hand. "Want to spend the rest of the night at my place?"

"Yeah." Sebastian gave him a tired smile. "But you should probably put your pants on before we go."

James laughed. "True. Can't have anyone else seeing the goods. They're only for you."

Sebastian preened, smiling fully now. "Damn right."

16

SEBASTIAN

A NOISE from downstairs woke Sebastian. He didn't know what it was. Was someone there? Had more people broken in to kidnap him? His heart pounded and he didn't know what to do.

Then he remembered he was at James's house and the person moving around downstairs was probably Eli or Parker.

He let out a long breath, trying to calm his panicked response. Sebastian reminded himself the whole town didn't hate him. A few bad people didn't mean he wasn't welcome here. Then he shook himself. Did it even matter? He was probably doomed to go down with the veins and here he was still trying to settle into his life.

Would he ever get that little house on a plot of land he'd envisioned last night?

James stirred next to him, groaning as he began to wake up. An arm wrapped around Sebastian's middle, and James pulled Sebastian close as if he was James's first thought and holding him was a desire that ran so deep James didn't even need to be fully awake to express it.

"Morning, sweetheart," James murmured in his ear, kissing his neck.

"Morning." Sebastian laced his fingers between James's, and they stayed like that, holding each other like nothing else mattered.

James kissed Sebastian's neck once more. "Ready to get up?"

"Sure." Sebastian wanted to stay in bed and hide from his problems, but it had gotten to the point that he wasn't sure anything, even James, could distract him properly.

He and James met Eli in the kitchen. Thankfully, coffee was already waiting. James had bought some powdered creamer for Sebastian, who couldn't stand the taste of half-and-half anymore. He smiled as he spooned it into his mug, even though his preference for the powdered stuff was a lingering Storm House habit.

"Parker is on the breakfast shift," Eli informed them as they sipped their coffee. "Would you guys come out to the vein intersection with me to get my data?"

James nodded. "We should check on the hole as well."

Sebastian put his mug down. "What if there are shades? We saw that hand, and after the one stealing Eli's backpack, we can't assume there'll be none around."

"We'll be on our guard," James promised. "But we can't let the shades keep us stuck inside doing nothing. Once we check things out, maybe we should see about getting another fuel cell to link to the curse. We can do the transfer spell again. Even if we can't recreate Selma's original spell, maybe it will help stabilize things."

Sebastian and Eli agreed. They might as well try.

An hour later, James pulled up to the Storm House gate. Sebastian spent some time with Miss Moo before heading to the clearing, James and Eli joining him rather than going ahead. The cow seemed happy enough out here by herself, even if she was overly excited to see Sebastian. Still, he'd be happier once he had a house with enough land to move her onto so he could see her more often.

No shades floated around the main part of the property, but

that didn't stop Sebastian from bracing himself as they entered the trees. He didn't relax the whole walk through the woods.

James stepped into the clearing ahead of Sebastian and Eli. "Um, guys…"

Eli pushed past, looking worried by the tone of James's voice. Sebastian stepped forward and paused, taking in the scene before them.

The hole was bigger, almost double what it had been last time. Sebastian swore something shimmery sat in the middle even though the hole was still dark as ink. It was hard to be sure, but the shadow at the center seemed to flicker.

There was nothing else in the clearing. The fuel cell was still by the path, but that was it. All of Eli's mechanisms were gone.

"The hole isn't big enough to swallow all my equipment." Eli spun to face him and James. "The mechanisms were all right along the edge, and that ground is solid. They were warded."

Sebastian had sympathy for Eli's frustration. Shades may have broken Parker's wards in town to smash the lights but everything out here had been left alone until now.

"Look." James pointed across the clearing where one of the blue tarps that had been covering the crates had been discarded at the base of a tree.

Eli rushed forward, but James grabbed him. "Careful."

They walked along the trees surrounding the clearing, a safe distance from the hole, until they reached the tarp.

Eli picked it up. "Why would the shades break through Parker's wards now? Did they decide to steal my bag and ruin everything all at once?"

"I don't know. I'm sorry, Eli," James said.

Sebastian spotted something glinting farther into the trees. He went to investigate and, upon reaching it, found a small piece of metal, then another a foot away.

He brought them back to the others and handed them to Eli. "Looks like pieces of a mechanism."

"They snapped it. Look." Eli's cheeks were red and his face twisted in fury. "Those black tendrils must be back. They seemed like the only things that could break wards."

"I wouldn't be surprised if that humanoid shade could break them as well." Sebastian grimaced at the thought. "Neither being back is good."

Eli threw the tarp on the ground, looking as frustrated as he was angry. "I can't have these kinds of setbacks. I need to be able to work to figure anything out."

Sebastian couldn't help wondering if it really was so much of a setback. They didn't necessarily need to monitor the energy flow in the veins anymore. It wouldn't tell them how to fix anything, but he didn't want to say so in case Eli took offense. He was only trying his best to help.

"If shades are trying to stop us from examining the veins, we must be on to something," Eli continued, his eyebrows pulled together like he was thinking hard.

"Or they're being territorial." Sebastian looked back toward the clearing. "That must be why they've always acted possessive around Storm House. They were guarding their gateway and must not have wanted me messing with it any more than they wanted you studying it, Eli."

Eli made an indignant sound. "So are we just going to let them have it?"

"No, they can't have the gateway." James placed a steadying hand on Eli's shoulder. "We need to access the intersection to hook up another fuel cell or whatever we end up doing to try and calm the imbalance. But maybe if the shades think we've stopped monitoring the veins, they'll back off a bit."

"Maybe," Eli agreed reluctantly. "I guess we should clean all this up. I'm sure pieces of my mechanisms are all over the place." He bent to pick up the tarp he'd tossed on the ground.

Sebastian and James helped, picking through the trees for the rest of the torn-apart equipment.

As he hunted around in the dirt, Sebastian's mind wandered. He tried to imagine what taking a piece of the vein would have looked like. How on earth had Sullivan and Nelson managed it? The vein was underground. Had they dug down to it? Could you even dig into a vein?

With the strange hole currently occupying the clearing, it was hard to imagine what the veins were like when they were whole. He'd always thought of energy flowing through the earth as a non-physical substance, not something you could see with the naked eye, but maybe the veins looked like a void similar to the hole.

When Sebastian had connected to the vein in town he hadn't had any sense of what it looked like, just that it was part of him and that he was in the earth.

The smell of decaying leaves and dirt suddenly overwhelmed Sebastian. His head pounded and he closed his eyes against the sun's glare. The earthy smell intensified, making him disoriented. Was he just hyperaware of the forest around him, or was this strange sensation something else?

James appeared at his side. "You okay?"

"Headache," Sebastian replied, voice strained, blinking against the light. "I was thinking about the veins and connecting to them, and it's like my memories triggered the pain…or triggered something."

"You're not trying to connect to them now, are you?"

"No." Sebastian was horrified at the thought. "Even if I'm the missing piece's stand-in, I don't think I'm supposed to harness the veins' power, or it wouldn't hurt so bad. I'm afraid of what connecting to the veins again might do to me."

"Me too," James confessed.

Something snagged in Sebastian's mind. He looked at the ominous hole in the clearing. "I had a funny vision when first connecting to the veins."

James cocked a brow. "You did?"

A swell of emotion rose up in Sebastian, making his heart ache in the worst way. "When I thought I couldn't save you, I lost all hope. I didn't think I could go on without you. It was too much. The shade had you and I'd failed. Everything was lost. It was over. I imagined myself dead and buried in the ground like I belonged there, and that's how I finally connected to the veins."

James's eyes shone with unshed tears. "Buried?" he choked.

Sebastian nodded, something even worse than remembering his hopeless wish to die turning his insides cold. "What if it wasn't just a random vision or me giving up?"

James's brow furrowed. "What do you mean?"

"What if I pictured being in the ground because I should be. What if I *do* belong. What if I'm enough of a stand-in for the missing piece to complete the veins."

James shook his head. "No, that's not... How could that be? You're linked to the veins already, and that's clearly not enough."

"I know, but what if I have to go back into the ground for it to be enough?" Sebastian whispered, the scent of decaying leaves washing over him anew.

James stood silent and Sebastian could practically hear his thoughts whirring as his frown grew even more severe. James eyed Sebastian like he'd never seen him before.

"*Back?* No, you were never there, Sebastian," James said at last. "I don't see how being in the earth would help. You're tied to the veins. Where you are physically shouldn't matter."

"I'm not so sure." Sebastian didn't want it to be true. He didn't want his vision of himself buried and no longer living to be some sort of premonition. But it felt right. It fit. This way, they could return the missing piece. It had been destroyed, but a new piece had been created. Except, the imbalance had never truly been solved because Sullivan never returned to the veins, never went into the ground to put it all back together.

"Sebastian." James grabbed his arm. "That can't be the answer. You aren't actually part of the veins. You're connected to them *like* a unit, *but you aren't actually one.* Going in to join them wouldn't do anything. The missing piece was made of natural energy. Your magic isn't the same. It doesn't add up the way you're thinking."

"Maybe not." Sebastian allowed himself to be relieved. "I honestly felt like I was losing my mind the night you were captured. Everything I was thinking was a mess. It just feels like it could all add up, you know?"

James gripped him harder. "We all want a neat solution, but that doesn't mean we'll get one. You're blood and bone, not pure magic. You're a stand-in only. We can't put the veins back together completely with you or anything else. This isn't the answer."

Sebastian nodded. He knew James didn't want to lose him any more than he wanted to lose James, but James's disagreement was more than him being in denial or getting caught up in wishful thinking. James had a point. Sebastian felt sure he'd figured it all out just now, but he had nothing to back it up other than gut feeling and conjecture. He told himself that meant he was wrong.

He wanted to be wrong. If he was right, that meant nothing good was ever going to last. For real, this time. Completing the veins would mean he'd lose everything, and he couldn't have that. He deserved good things. This curse wasn't allowed to take his life from him.

But the fear that it would creeped back in. He'd always felt doomed, hadn't he?

Jᴀᴍᴇꜱ ʜᴇʟᴅ Sebastian's hand tight as they left the clearing. His heart broke to hear Sebastian had gone through such a low point, thinking he'd lost James, but he was glad Sebastian had shared it with him.

Eli hurried ahead as they walked like he sensed their need for some space. James was grateful for the privacy.

"You know you always have something to live for," he whispered as they walked.

"I know." Sebastian squeezed James's hand.

"If you ever get those feelings again, there's always help."

Sebastian paused, facing James. "I don't think I'll ever be in that place again. Really. But if I do ever find myself thinking dying is my best option, I'll reach out."

James sensed Sebastian meant it, except that didn't help much when Sebastian also thought he could literally fill the hole the missing piece had created in the veins. "So this idea that you could fulfill your vision and fix everything isn't related to wanting to die?"

"No." Sebastian shook his head. "I don't want to join the stupid veins in the earth. It just felt like all the puzzle pieces fit together. I don't *want* them to. I want my life more than anything." He sounded adamant, like a man willing to fight.

"Good." James kissed Sebastian, then pulled him along to catch up with Eli.

"We need to do something though." Sebastian's grim demeanor returned. "We can't wait around and let things escalate further."

"I know." James glanced from Sebastian to Eli and back again, thinking. "Let's take one of the fuel cells from Gray's and transfer the curse to it. We can do it now."

Sebastian stopped. "Not if anyone might drive by the property."

Even though it was a reminder of his parents' accident, James's heart warmed. Sebastian always looked out for other people. He was kind to his core, even when others didn't return that kindness.

James gave Sebastian a reassuring smile. "We'll get Eleanor to close the road. There's plenty of advantages to having her in the know, and I'm not coming back here at night, so we're making use of everything we've got."

Sebastian nodded, looking relieved as some of the tension left his body.

"What happened to leading the shades to believe we've abandoned messing with the veins?" Eli asked.

"Dealing with shades isn't our primary issue," Sebastian said. "It'd be great if they left us alone but we have to put fixing the veins first."

Eli fell into step beside them. "Don't get me wrong, I agree. It just makes it harder having shades messing with us. I wish there was a way to get them to leave us alone."

They continued on, passing the small cemetery, when movement caught James's eye. A figure stood at the back of the fenced-in plot under the shadowy canopy of the trees.

James stopped short. Everything was unnaturally dark around

the looming shadow, making it hard to see clearly even though the cemetery was on the edge of the forest and shouldn't have been darker than the trees they'd just left.

"Sebastian," James hissed.

Both Sebastian and Eli turned, and the figure came into focus. They all stared at the large humanoid shade Sebastian had banished barely a week ago. At least James assumed it was the same being. There was no way to tell if it was another individual of the same shade species since it had no discerning features, but instinct told him it was the same one that had abducted him.

Sebastian sucked in a breath beside James.

They couldn't fight this damn shade, not now. Sebastian had nearly killed himself with the effort last time.

James herded the other two along, hurrying up the path. They seemed to shake themselves from their shock and moved quickly. James glanced over his shoulder to see how fast the shade was gaining on them, but it hadn't moved. The giant figure remained behind the graves. The next time James looked, he saw it fading away, deeper into the forest in the opposite direction.

"It's leaving," he told the others.

They ran to his truck anyway.

JAMES PULLED INTO GRAY ELECTRICAL. He was much more apprehensive about dragging one of his fuel cells out to Storm House now.

"Why did it let us walk away?" Sebastian asked, not moving to get out of the truck after Eli, who stood in the driveway on his phone, likely talking to Parker.

"I don't know." James's hand shook. He shoved it through his hair to fend off the tremors. He might not remember being captured by the formidable shade, but knowing it had happened was terrifying enough.

"I assumed it'd bring the darkness back when it returned, but it seems like it's waiting for something."

"Or tying out new tactics," James countered. "Come on, we can't just sit here."

They got out of the truck and went inside the shop. Hazel and Eleanor were by the coffee maker, heads together as they spoke in low voices.

"Great, you're here. We need to talk to you," James called across the room.

Both women looked up, and James told them about the humanoid shade they'd just seen.

"Just what we fucking need," Eleanor muttered. She looked more harried than James had ever seen her, her tidy professional appearance lacking its usual air of perfection. "William is MIA."

"What?" Sebastian crossed his arms and glared. "He has to be in Moonlight Falls somewhere."

"Well, the police can't find him, and as far as I know, no one's admitted to seeing him since yesterday evening."

James perched on the edge of his desk. "What about the other guys who broke into Sebastian's place?"

"They're giving the Apple Valley Police Department a major headache. They were arrested, but when the officers couldn't leave Moonlight Falls with them, they assumed Jim and the other culprits were using magic to try and avoid being taken to jail. I think they're being placed under house arrest until an official with magical expertise can come assist the police."

"I hope they don't send the same official who wouldn't come into town during the darkness," Hazel muttered.

"They probably are." Eleanor scowled before turning to Sebastian. "You'll need to make a statement if you're going to press charges."

Sebastian grimaced. "Sure, but that's far from my top priority right now."

Eleanor gave him an understanding look.

"We need to close North Road so we can link another fuel cell to the veins," James explained. "Can we get city maintenance to put up cones and monitor the road so no one goes through?"

Eleanor gave a tired nod. "I'll make a call. Kitty heard about the veins, so at least I won't have to come up with an excuse. I'm sure she can get a team up there today."

James stood and paced the workroom. This was good. They were making progress. He just didn't know what they'd do if that humanoid shade was still in the woods at Storm House.

The shop door banged open and James whirled around. Samantha Storm stood in the doorway, cheeks red and hair disheveled.

"Sebastian." She stomped across the shop and rounded the counter.

James stepped in her path.

"What did you do?" she growled, trying to sidestep James, glaring at her son.

Sebastian shrank back. The look of shock he'd worn at the first sight of his mother turned into hurt. "I didn't do anything."

"Yes, you did." Samantha turned her glare on James. "Excuse me."

James put out an arm, grabbing the counter and completely blocking Samantha's path to the back of the shop. "No. You can stand right here and explain what you're yelling about."

She slammed her handbag down on the counter. "I'm trapped. That's what I'm yelling about. So, Sebastian, what did you do?"

"Nothing," he said more forcefully than before. "Unlike you, I don't trap people on purpose."

"Then why can't I get out of Moonlight Falls?" Samantha asked desperately.

James didn't have any pity for the woman's plight. Out of

everyone to get caught up in this mess, she was the only one to deserve it. However, he was confused as to how it'd happened. Samantha had known about the curse for decades, so her being trapped wasn't like all the townspeople who'd learned the secret and been claimed by the morphing curse on the unstable veins.

"I shouldn't be trapped here," Sebastian's mother insisted. "I didn't break the secret-binding. Sebastian, why are you trapped here even after you escaped the house? What's holding us in this town?"

Sebastian came up behind James, and he lowered the arm blocking Samantha. She didn't try to push past, just stared at her son.

"The veins are holding us here. We're trapped in the area bound by the length and width of the two intersecting branches."

Her look turned accusing. "Did you know I would be stuck when you saw me yesterday?"

"No." Sebastian wasn't trying to hide his hurt. You could see it plainly on his face and hear it in his voice. "The curse is changing. We added a new energy source to the veins and the area expanded, but ever since shades have started using the veins for otherworldly magic, things have been falling apart."

Samantha's nostrils flared.

"Everyone who knows the secret is stuck here. Seems that includes you." James frowned at her, the emotions he'd suppressed the last time he'd seen the woman winning out at last. "And, you know, maybe it's karma."

Samantha's face went scarlet. *"Excuse me?"*

James's own anger rose to the surface. "Karma paying you back for everything you've done. I know you and Stephen caused my parents' car accident." His voice caught, but he pressed on. "You killed them the night you damned your son and have tried to avoid the consequences of your actions ever since. Looks like your time is up."

Samantha stared at him in horror. There was no way she

hadn't known her spell had caused the accident. She wasn't shocked. She looked guilty.

Her eyes darted to Sebastian. "There's no proof. You can't hold me accountable for that."

"We don't need proof," Hazel said from the back of the room, coming to James's defense.

Samantha was startled like she hadn't realized anyone else was with them.

"You're right. James can't prove you caused the accident," Hazel continued. "But we know the truth, and so do you, and now you're stuck here with us."

Samantha took a step back. "It was still an accident. By the time we realized what happened, it had been days. There was no taking it back."

Admitting her part in the accidental deaths wasn't an apology, but James didn't want one. He'd never considered her part in the accident her biggest crime. "And what about cursing Sebastian? Was that an accident?" he growled.

"I thought we already covered the fact that I'm a terrible person," Samantha snapped.

"Mom, please." Sebastian rubbed his head like it was starting to hurt. "We have enough problems without arguing about this. If you aren't going to help, please just go away."

Samantha opened her mouth, then snapped it shut. She gathered her handbag and left the shop.

"The number of people I don't want to be trapped with keeps growing," Sebastian muttered.

James was impressed that Sebastian had managed to stay so calm in front of his mother. James's pulse was pounding. He'd expressed his anger but wasn't sure how much it had helped.

Dealing with Samantha Storm felt like a waste of energy. It wouldn't bring his parents back and wouldn't help Sebastian feel less abandoned or take away his years of loneliness. They needed to heal and move on from these things, not dwell on them, and the key to that didn't lie with Samantha.

Part of James was still pleased the woman was trapped. Call him vindictive. He didn't care. He liked to think there was at least some justice in the world. Her fate was tied to Sebastian now. If they were all going down, she'd be dragged along with them.

Eli entered the silent shop, breaking the tension. "That looked unpleasant. Did I miss anything crucial?"

"No," Sebastian said. "Don't worry about it."

"Okay, cool. But you should probably know three shades just flew down the street toward the center of town."

18

JAMES

James and Sebastian joined Eli by the door, looking out the window. They couldn't see the shades from here but James didn't doubt Eli's word.

Eleanor came up behind them. "We have to do something about shades being out in full sunlight." Her determination didn't quite cover the worried edge to her voice. "Not everyone can summon fire to fight them off. The town isn't safe with beasts like this flying around. Not when they've become so aggressive. I hesitated to put out an emergency alert about it yesterday when there was only one, but I'm regretting that, especially since that humanoid shade is back."

"Let's put an alert out now," Hazel suggested. "And report it while we're at it."

"I'll take a picture of a shade out in broad daylight and send it to the officials." Eleanor pursed her lips. "Perhaps *proof* will prompt them to send someone competent and willing to help."

James moved out of the doorway so Eleanor and Hazel could leave the shop. "Be careful out there."

"You too." Hazel grabbed his arm. "Are you still taking one of the fuel cells to Storm House?"

James nodded, and with that, the two women left, heading for town hall.

James turned to Eli. "Where's Parker?"

"Still at work."

"You might want to hang out at the diner until he gets off." James hated leaving Eli, but there was no way he was bringing him back to Storm House when they'd just seen that powerful shade by the cemetery.

"Yeah, okay." Eli scrunched his nose as if he didn't like James's implying he needed protecting, but James was glad he didn't argue.

The three of them exited the shop, and James locked up.

"I'll see you guys soon." Eli turned to head toward the diner.

"Wait," James called. "I'll drive you."

"It's only a block," Eli muttered.

"You just saw shades drifting by," Sebastian said gently. "And we think they're targeting you because of your research. It's not safe to be wandering around, even for a short distance."

"That's fair." Eli followed Sebastian to James's truck without another word.

James was grateful Sebastian had spoken up. He knew Eli got frustrated with his overprotectiveness, but in their current situation, was there such a thing as overprotective? James would rather annoy Eli than leave him open to any unnecessary risks. He'd drop Eli off, then come back for the fuel cell.

James pulled out of the Gray Electrical driveway, his unease growing. Something didn't feel right, and he could have sworn it was more than the stress of everything they were dealing with. He turned into the town circle and looked toward the diner.

A car was stopped in the middle of the road, all its windows smashed. No people were inside or around the scene, so they must have fled. Only a single shade hovered above the wreckage.

"Shit," muttered Sebastian.

James had hoped the shades Eli had seen had only been

passing through. The one yesterday hadn't been too disruptive. Seems that was wishful thinking.

The shade turned, its attention fixing on James's truck. James hit the gas, speeding around the wrecked car and past the park, where two more shades lurked. "I'm going to drive around to get to the parking lot from the other entrance."

"Good idea." Sebastian craned his neck, looking back at the smashed car. "Doesn't seem like the shades are following, so maybe they won't notice us behind the diner."

James white-knuckled the steering wheel. "I should be relieved they aren't following, but it only makes me suspicious."

"Me too," Sebastian agreed. Eli remained quiet.

James turned off Main Street and circled back to the diner's rear parking lot. He wondered if it was safe to leave Eli here. Yes, Parker was inside, but he was only one man, and who knew if the shades hovering around would leave or if more would join them.

James parked only to hesitate getting out.

Eli shifted nervously next to James. "I liked it better when this kind of stuff only happened at night."

James gave his brother a small smile. "Me too."

"It was definitely better back then, not that I'd have said so at the time." Sebastian opened his door. "Come on, let's all go in."

James followed suit, keeping an eye on the trees behind the park. If more shades were coming, they'd probably slip out of the shadows there.

A shout of alarm came from the other side of the truck.

James raced around, forgetting the trees. A shade had its arms wrapped around Sebastian's legs.

"It came out from under the truck." Eli pointed a shade-light at the beast, his hand shaking. The light did nothing, but it was all Eli could do without magic.

James shot sparks at the shade, but instead of them finding their mark, the shade disappeared. Like full-on disappeared, not dispersed into shadow as they usually did when leaving their solid form behind.

Sebastian whirled around. "Where did it go?"

"Come on." James reached for him. Where it went didn't matter. He'd rather get away than try to hunt it down.

Eli was already at the diner's back door, holding it open. As James and Sebastian reached it, the shade reappeared. It lunged for them but wasn't quick enough. They were past the diner's wards and out of its reach.

Eli closed the door in the beast's face. "Let's find Parker." He led them through the back and into the kitchen, but no one was there.

James pushed through the door to the front of the restaurant. Parker and Luna were looking out the front window along with Princeton Taylor, the museum curator who must have been in for an early lunch.

"What's going on?" Sebastian asked.

"We're watching the shade destruction." Parker turned to face them as Eli surged forward. He wrapped his arms around Parker, and Parker kissed the top of his head.

Princeton pressed a hand over his heart. "I've never seen anything like this. They're vicious, to say nothing of them being out on a bright day."

Sebastian shifted closer to James. Out the window, the shades had abandoned the park and the smashed car for the stone in the center. They darted around it but couldn't seem to get within a couple of feet of it.

"We need a good flamethrower to get rid of them," Parker mused, sounding like he was only half joking.

"Don't have one though, do we?" Luna responded, fully serious. "What are we going to do? I can't just sit in here watching. My daughter is at school just down the road. What if they fly off there next?"

"I'll call the school and warn them." Princeton pulled out his phone.

"Not to add to the issue, but one out back just disappeared like it could teleport," James said.

Parker turned to face him. "So these shades can withstand the sun and have more magical abilities than the ones we're used to. Great."

A shade appeared out of thin air on the other side of the glass, right in front of Luna. She gasped, taking a step back.

"Should I go out and set it on fire?" Parker asked the room at large.

"There's not many." James turned to Sebastian, thinking aloud. "If we can get rid of these ones, maybe we'll be good for a while."

"Or more will come, and we'll be caught in a fight out of our control," Sebastian countered.

Parker scowled out the window. "What else can we do, go home and hide?"

Eli looked up at Parker, who still held him close. "To be honest, that doesn't sound terrible." He seemed worried, and after how badly Parker drained himself last time, James wasn't surprised.

James pushed his own worries away. He couldn't let them cloud his judgment. He'd do anything to keep Sebastian, his brother, and his friends safe, but he couldn't let his fear affect his decision-making. He couldn't let it make him reckless.

Luna pulled a purse from behind the counter. "I'm going to head out. I don't feel comfortable so close to shades I can't fend off." She glanced at Parker, who nodded his acknowledgment.

"The school is calling parents," Princeton said, rejoining the conversation now that his phone call had ended. "They'll keep everyone inside until the end of the school day, but if people want to collect their kids early, they can."

"Good, that's exactly what I was planning to do." Luna took

off her apron and stuffed it in her bag. "I don't know what's going on with Moonlight Falls. First that darkness, then this."

"Don't worry about your shifts if you want to get out of town," Parker assured her. "In fact, I'd recommend leaving for a while."

Luna looked relieved. "Thanks, I might just do that."

Parker walked her out to make sure there wasn't anything lurking in the parking lot.

The shade on the other side of the front window seemed to be inspecting the building. It studied the glass, swooping around to all corners, but didn't seem to be looking inside the diner. The shades by the stone continued to dart around, their movements giving off an increasing air of agitation.

James and Sebastian exchanged a weary look.

Parker returned, slipping an arm around Eli. "I think I'll close up." He turned to the diner's sole customer. "Sorry, Princeton, but getting out of town might be best. Unless you want to risk a confrontation with one of these beasts."

"No, I don't want to risk that." Princeton frowned. "But I'm parked out by the post office. Hell, I never thought I'd be nervous walking across the street in broad daylight."

The shade at the window turned abruptly and flew toward the ones circling the stone. Instead of joining in the frantic flying, it hovered above them. In response, the three stopped circling and drifted up to the newcomer.

"It's like they're communicating," Princeton muttered, transfixed by the shades. "Only it doesn't look like their mouths are moving at all. Could they be telepathic? I'd always thought their chattering and shrieking was how they talked to one another."

James remembered how the humanoid shade had spoken and the way its voice seemed to fill his mind rather than the air around him. It very well could have been some sort of telepathic ability.

Suddenly, all four shades disappeared, not leaving so much as a whisp of shadow behind.

"Shit." Princeton let out a surprised laugh. "There's my chance. Best of luck to you all." He darted out the front door and hurried across the circle, disappearing into the post office, presumably to get to his car parked out back.

Parker flipped the sign on the door to Closed, turned off the neon Open sign displayed in the window, and locked the front door.

"Should we head home?" Eli asked.

"James and I are still going to Storm House." Sebastian glanced at James. "Right?"

"Yeah." He gripped Sebastian's shoulder. "But all four of us don't need to go."

Parker opened his mouth, most likely to argue, but a commotion outside stole his attention.

Shades reappeared around the stone. One screeched, and they all charged the rock, only to be held back by Parker's ward, unable to touch it.

"Good thing you suggested we protect it," Eli said to Sebastian. "Maybe they can't bring the darkness back without it."

A sound like the heater knocking came from above their heads. James looked up. It happened again, and he swore the ceiling shook.

Sebastian pressed against him. "What…?"

A vent over the counter rattled as a black shadow poured out of it, looking less like smoke and more like ink spilling into a glass of water.

James and Sebastian shot sparks at it simultaneously. The ink-black shadow burst briefly into flame before dissipating, sent back to Beyond.

Parker pulled Eli behind him. How had the shade gotten through? Had something been on the roof, working to break the wards this whole time they were standing around?

"Where does the heating system pull air into the building?" Sebastian asked.

"Out back." Parker scrubbed a hand over his face. "Shit. They probably broke in back there. I should go repair the ward."

No sooner had the words left his mouth than more inky shadow poured out of the vent. James struck again. At least it was easy to banish shades when they were confined to one narrow entrance to the room.

Parker pushed past into the kitchen, Eli in tow.

Sebastian grabbed James's arm. "There's a hell of a lot more of them outside now."

Another shade came through the vent, and James banished it. He didn't want to look away in case more came in. "What's happening, Sebastian?"

"There's got to be a half-dozen shades around the stone, and something's coming out of the ground."

"The ground?" James asked in alarm, just as another shadow appeared in the vent.

"Oh fuck." Sebastian squeezed James's arm. "It's those tendril things. They're swarming the stone."

James turned to look. "Should we abandon the diner and try to fight them off instead? The stone is obviously important if they're going after the wards on it."

Worry creased Sebastian's brow. "I don't know if I can defeat the tendrils without using the veins. You have to find the center to kill the whole thing."

"Ah, shit." Just in time, James noticed a shade that had gotten all the way through the vent and was returning to solid form. He quickly banished it. "I wish we'd left when Princeton did."

Parker and Eli burst back through the kitchen door. "Wards are secured. You wanna head out?" His last word faded as he looked out the front window.

Eli's eyes widened. "Let's not go that way."

The tendrils had completely covered the stone. Did that mean the humanoid shade was nearby? It seemed to pop up along with the tendrils. Both clearly had more powerful magic than other shades.

A thundering sound interrupted James's thoughts. Deer streamed out of the woods and through the park into the street. Several stags were among them, rearing on their back legs, unnaturally black eyes glinting. They surrounded the grass where the stone was being swarmed by the tendrils, the largest ones continuing to gallop around the street, tossing their heads.

James was speechless. There was no sense going out there to try and save the stone now. They should run out back, get in the truck and leave.

An SUV drove into the north side of the circle, slamming on its brakes as the driver noticed the strange spectacle in the middle of the road. A truck stopped behind it. James willed them to turn and drive away.

Sebastian and Eli made simultaneous sounds of apprehension. This wouldn't be good, but James couldn't make himself look away. He was rooted to the spot. Maybe he should help, but he couldn't rid himself of the feeling that going outside would only hurt him and everyone he was with.

The largest stag broke away from the herd and charged the SUV, ramming its antlers into the front of the vehicle. Sebastian jolted beside James. The stag pulled its antlers from the dented metal and threw its head back, mouth open to expose pointy onyx teeth, as it let out a high-pitched shriek.

A chill ran down James's spine. The people in those vehicles needed to get the hell out of there. Instead, two men jumped out of the truck behind the SUV.

"Oh my god, Sam!" Eli shouted as his old childhood friend reached into the back of the truck.

The other man was Sam's father, Carson Lee. The logging crew must have come back to town early, which on its own didn't bode well for what might be happening out in the forest.

Carson leveled a hunting rifle at the stag and shot twice, once in the chest and once in the head. The possessed animal jolted and dropped like a stone, the shade bursting from its body to be destroyed by the sunlight.

The other deer took notice. Three more stags charged the cars. The SUV surged forward, hitting one and knocking it down. Sam had his own rifle and took aim at another. His first shot sent it to the ground, his second killing it and destroying the shade as Carson took care of the last stag.

The stag that the SUV had just hit to the ground got to its feet and went straight for Sam, showing no signs that the vehicle impact had hurt it even though it was bleeding. Sam seemed transfixed, a look of fear on his face as the bloody stag bared its unnatural razor-sharp teeth.

Carson took the beast down just in time. It fell at Sam's feet, the shade possessing it shrieking as it was destroyed.

"Fuck," Sebastian breathed, a hand over his mouth.

The rest of the deer bolted for the woods, the shades possessing them probably unwilling to risk being shot and banished back to Beyond.

With all the commotion, James had lost track of the tendrils around the stone. When he looked back, the writhing mass was gone. Shades caressed the stone with their hands, no longer held back by Parker's wards.

"What do we do?" Eli whispered, gaze fixed on the stone.

"Get the hell out of here." Sebastian turned to go out the back, but James grabbed him as the shades around the stone vanished into thin air.

"Wait." James still couldn't look away, like watching and knowing what was happening helped somehow. Where had the shades gone?

Carson and Sam got back in their truck, and the two vehicles tore out of the town center, leaving the deer where they lay in the street. At least the Lees weren't trapped and could get out of town along with Luna and Princeton. James hoped the rest of the crew was free too.

"Should I re-ward the stone?" Parker asked, sounding unsure.

"Unless we have a way of guarding the ward, I don't know if it's worth the effort," James admitted. "With the shades set on breaking it, they're bound to do it again."

"It's probably best to save your strength for wards that will keep you safe," Sebastian added.

Parker turned away from the window. "In that case, let's go."

19

SEBASTIAN

Sebastian tried to ignore the headache building behind his eyes as he followed James and the others out to the back of the diner.

Parker locked up the rear door and slung an arm around Eli, keeping him close. "You'll meet us back at my place when you're done at Storm House?" Parker directed the question at James, sounding reluctant to separate.

"We'll go straight there," James promised. "And if you can, call Hazel and let them know—" A human-sounding shout interrupted him. Strangely, it wasn't one of fear.

Another shout, almost like a whoop, came from the direction of the woods. An answering cheer followed.

Parker paused on the way to his car. "What the devil?"

Sebastian turned his attention from the park to James. "Didn't the deer all run that way? I can't imagine someone being happy about that if they were in the trees."

James couldn't seem to find words. Stress lined his face and he wore a scowl so determined Sebastian feared for anything that stood in his way.

He was struck by how much he loved James. Not just when things were good and they were whispering sweet nothings in

149

each other's ears, but always. He loved this loyal, protective, and unassumingly fierce man. He loved James for his strengths and his fears and trusted James to stand by him like no one else.

Sebastian wanted to grab James and kiss him. Wanted to push him up against the truck and fuck him, show anyone who cared to look that their love wouldn't be beaten down by anything, from this world or Beyond.

He wished they lived in a reality where they could have done that. Instead, William burst out of the woods, almost as unwelcome a sight as shades during the day.

William stopped short at the sight of Sebastian, James, Parker, and Eli standing in the parking lot. He blinked oddly, making Sebastian wonder if something was wrong with his eyes.

More people came crashing through the trees. Sebastian recognized two of the men from the break-in at the duplex standing at the front of the small crowd. A jolt of fear coursed through him.

William appeared to collect himself. He pointed at Sebastian. "Look who it is. This might be perfect."

"I don't think so." Parker took a step forward, putting himself between Sebastian and the crowd.

"You're a wanted man, William," James warned, venom in his tone, as his arm settled securely around Sebastian.

The touch would have been more comforting if Sebastian's chest wasn't so tight. The whole crowd glared at him like they hated him.

The men who'd broken into his place were supposed to be under house arrest, other than William, who'd evaded capture. They'd obviously escaped, but what had happened to the officers guarding them? And where had these other people come from? Even with the mess of the Storm House secret getting out, Sebastian had wanted to believe that most people would understand once Eleanor set them straight.

William ignored James's warning, turning to the man beside

him. "Take a few people and grab the ginger." He addressed the rest of the crowd. "The rest of you stay with me. It's time to rid this town of useless leaders who think imprisonment is acceptable."

The group shouted in agreement, and William marched off, followed by six others. Those that remained continued to glare. One of the men who'd broken into his house leered at Sebastian.

His head throbbed. A literal mob was coming for him. Their scrutiny and judgmental expressions were like a crushing weight, feeding his anxiety as the undisguised hatred on display brought to life some of Sebastian's worst fears.

It had been bad enough worrying people judged him or found him annoying and unlikeable before. He'd had enough trouble being around groups that, rationally, he'd known weren't paying attention to him. In comparison, this situation was impossible. It wasn't fair and made Sebastian so angry he was getting light-headed, though that could just be from his growing headache.

Parker took another step in front of Sebastian. "Anyone who comes closer is going to regret it."

"Piss off, Hayes," someone spat.

"Not likely, Mills. I'm the one with all the magic. Half of you don't even have the ability. Go home. You can't take us by physical force. James and I would beat you at that, even without extra power."

Sebastian had a wild thought that he was grateful the mob didn't have pitchforks or other weapons. He gripped James tight, wanting to sink away from this and disappear while also wanting to rage at these people and fight back.

Parker's words seemed to sink in. Some of the people glanced around in hesitation.

"This isn't going to work."

"But he's the real problem. Screw Eleanor. William just wants her out of the way so he can be mayor."

Beside Sebastian, James muttered a spell. Wind whipped

safely around Parker and Eli and hit the crowd. The people in the front took the brunt of the blast and toppled into those behind them.

"We've got more important things to do than deal with this," James snarled. "Shades are attacking during the day. Why don't you try to do something about that? You should all be ashamed of yourselves."

The animosity in the air seemed to hit a peak. Sebastian worried the mob was about to attack, then someone said, "Fuck it, we were supposed to be going to town hall. If William wants Storm, he can get him himself."

Another voice shouted agreement, and they hurried out of the park.

Sebastian watched them go but found no relief. "That isn't any better than them going after me. We have to help Eleanor and Hazel."

"You're right." James ran a hand roughly through his hair. "We need to shut this down quickly."

Parker looked down at Eli. "You good to come along?"

The younger man nodded. Sebastian could tell James and Parker were displeased about dragging Eli into danger when he didn't have the advantage of magic, but at least this was only human danger. For now. Sebastian doubted the shades would be absent from the center of town for long now that the stone was free.

Why couldn't William leave them alone?

Sebastian didn't want to go after the mob. His stomach was already twisted in knots and his hands were shaking, but he couldn't sit by while they went after Eleanor. It wasn't lost on him that, in many ways, it had been easier to face a horde of shades than a mob of angry people. But he had friends in his corner, and with James beside him, he could face any horribleness the world threw at him.

Sebastian's heart thudded as he rounded the diner, glued to James's side. They marched across the road, ignoring the stone.

On the steps of town hall, the administrator who usually sat at the reception desk was blocking the entrance to the ruined foyer, a look of determined anger on his face. "You all need to leave town. An evacuation notice has been put out for Moonlight Falls. Didn't you see the shades?"

"Get out of the way, Jay," William growled from the front of the mob.

"You've been fired," the administrator, Jay, shot back, tone full of authority. "Don't tell me what to do."

William laughed, and the sound made the hair on the back of Sebastian's neck stand up. It must have unsettled Jay as well. He took a step back, his confidence cracking.

Eleanor and Hazel appeared in the doorway behind Jay. Eleanor wore an absolutely lethal expression. She stepped in front of Jay, releasing a gust of wind on the crowd. People stumbled back around William while he managed to remain unaffected.

James led the way, pushing through the people, Sebastian close on his heels with Parker and Eli at his back. They came to stand next to Eleanor and Hazel.

William's nostrils flared, his eyes finding Sebastian. He shuddered, almost like he was cold. It was weird, given the day was perfectly nice for the season. Even his glare seemed to flicker, but he collected himself, saying, "Seems I have to do everything myself."

"Authorities are on their way," Eleanor interrupted before William could say more.

"Oh? And how'd that work for you last time?" William cocked his head. "Besides, I've got an hour before anyone gets here from Apple Valley. The town has had enough of you, Eleanor. You're not fit to look after Moonlight Falls when you're more interested in protecting the cause of our problems than fixing them." His gaze settled on Sebastian.

Another chill coursed through Sebastian as his headache flared. He gripped James's arm to steady himself, trying to ignore the angry crowd. William was bad enough on his own. Even his eyes looked strangely evil.

Sebastian hated all of this. He didn't want to deal with it, especially not when he and James should have been back at Storm House by now.

"The only one causing problems here is you," Sebastian said, surprised at how steady his voice was given his insides were in knots.

William bared his teeth at Sebastian, making an almost hissing sound.

Eleanor's eyes widened at the strange display.

"There would have been nothing wrong if you'd stayed out of our business." William ascended the town hall steps. "Everything would have gone to plan."

"Plan?" Eleanor walked down the steps to meet him. "What the hell are you talking about?"

William's gaze jerked away from Sebastian. "This isn't your town anymore, Eleanor."

"It was never *my* town. I'm the mayor, not the fucking king of the castle."

William didn't appear to be listening. He made a grab for Eleanor's wrist. As if the move had been a signal to the crowd, they rushed forward.

Eleanor unleashed another gust of wind, stronger than the last. It halted the mob for a moment, but then William was on her.

A stab of pain shot through Sebastian's head, and he lost track of what was happening around him. He felt sick. Why did he have to get his worst headache since using the veins now? He was useless. Forget standing by Eleanor. He was a liability.

James held him tight, and when the pain passed and Sebastian opened his eyes, it was James's face that filled his vision.

"What's wrong?"

Sebastian didn't know. Something was coming, but he had no idea how he knew that.

Shouts echoed around them. Something tugged on Sebastian's sleeve. He tore his eyes from James to find one of the angry Moonlighters clinging to his arm, trying to pull him down the steps. Sebastian wobbled, off-balance. James was the only thing keeping him from falling.

Without thinking, Sebastian said the words for fire. The man's jacket caught around the cuff. He shouted, and Sebastian felt a flash of horror. It was fine using fire on shades to banish them, but this was someone living.

The man whipped off his jacket and stomped on it, putting out the flames. His wrist was red and his eyes were full of hatred as he looked up at Sebastian. "Motherfucker," he growled but didn't reach for Sebastian again.

Not that Sebastian was in the clear. More men pushed past the burned one, surrounding him and James. Eleanor, Hazel, Parker, and Eli were surrounded too, though it seemed Eleanor had escaped William. Their fight had turned physical. Someone grabbed Hazel from behind, and Eleanor shoved them off.

"We have to use magic," James said as he pushed someone off him. He seemed to catch Parker's eye, and the two nodded at each other. Simultaneously, they sent wind rushing outward. The gust burst forth, knocking everyone who wasn't holding on to James or Parker down.

Parker caught Hazel, and Eleanor managed to steady Eli. Everyone else tumbled down the steps or was thrown back into the town hall behind them.

It wasn't enough. People got up, looking madder than before. It didn't look like anything short of injury would deter them.

A shriek came from the other side of the circle but half the people seemed to ignore it.

Sebastian looked over his shoulder and swore, pulling James away from a person making another pass at him. "Shades!" They'd stayed in town too long, and the beasts were back.

Shadows stirred in the park. A mass of shades rushed out of the woods, flooding the street. Shouts rang up from the mob, but they were no longer full of anger. People panicked. Perhaps they'd missed the emergency alert about shades powerful enough to be out in broad daylight and hadn't believed James's warning.

The swarm of shades circled the stone. Sebastian almost thought they'd ignore all the people in favor of their obsession with the rock, but onyx eyes fixed on them. Sebastian could have sworn they'd fixed on him specifically.

Some of the shades raced across the street toward town hall. The mob ran, abandoning him and Eleanor. A few people reached the door to town hall and pulled on the handle, but it must have been locked. Jay was nowhere to be seen, so perhaps he'd hidden inside.

William knocked into Sebastian. He seemed to be struggling to follow the others. William looked over his shoulder at the approaching shades and fear flashed across his face before it disappeared. He stepped away from the rest of the mob, which was now running around to the back of the building.

Sebastian shook himself. "We have to run," he called to the others. The charging shades had followed the mob, but that didn't mean they weren't coming back.

James guided Sebastian down the steps toward the shades around the stone, but they had to go that way to get to their vehicles. None of the beasts had attacked, so maybe they were content to chase everyone out of the town center.

Something gripped the back of Sebastian's hoodie, causing the collar to choke him as he was pulled backward, hand slipping from James's grip.

"I don't think so," William rasped in his ear. There was something wrong with his voice.

Sebastian wrenched his hoodie out of the man's hands, spinning around to face him. Two shades floated on either side of William. Sebastian balked at how close the beasts were and the fact that William not only showed no signs of fear but hardly seemed to notice.

"I can't let you out of my sight," William rumbled.

"Sebastian, come on." James was at his side, trying to pull him away. "You aren't imprisoning Sebastian at Storm House, William. Just lay off."

William blinked and his eyes went black, whites completely gone. He smiled, showing razor-sharp onyx teeth.

20

SEBASTIAN

SEBASTIAN'S HEAD pounded as he held the shade's stare. He'd never heard of one possessing a human before.

William's deadly smile turned to a sneer. James staggered back in shock.

"I don't want you at Storm House," the William-shade said, solid black eyes glinting. "I want you where I can keep an eye on you."

William's human motives with the mob had been clear. This wasn't. Why would the shade possessing him want to keep an eye on Sebastian?

Sebastian had lost track of Parker and the others. James seemed stunned where he stood, like the possessed person was too much to process. Sebastian needed to get James the hell out of there. He stepped toward James, but William's hands clamped down on Sebastian's right arm, yanking him to the side.

He stumbled, and the shades beside William swooped in on James. Sebastian tried and failed to pull free from William's vice-like grip. William had him off-balance, and with a shove, Sebastian found himself on the ground.

William's face leaned in close as he twisted Sebastian's arm behind his back. "We will not let you make the sacrifice necessary to bar us from this world," he hissed in a voice that didn't sound human. "We have been called, and we will claim this place as our own."

"W-what?" Sebastian sputtered, momentarily forgetting all his fear as confusion overtook him.

William yelled in pain and his face disappeared from Sebastian's sight. Sebastian's arm was released, and he pushed himself up.

Parker held William by the hair. He kicked the possessed man in the back of the legs, and he crumpled forward, knees hitting the pavement.

James stood beside Parker, breathing hard. Blood dripped from a scratch on his cheek. The two shades that had attacked him seemed to have been banished.

William shrieked and thrashed, the noises coming out of him purely animalistic. The shades around the stone turned at the sound, letting out returned cries of outrage.

"Fuck, we need to get the shade out of him," James said.

"Wait." Sebastian stepped in front of the struggling William-shade. "What did you mean? What sacrifice to bar you from this world?"

The shade snapped its onyx teeth, saliva running down William's chin. "Sacrifice is how magic works in the world of blood and bone, is it not?"

The humanoid shade had planned to sacrifice James to cement its hold on Moonlight Falls. Did that mean…?

Shades swarmed Sebastian, James, and Parker. The ones from the stone must have decided to attack after all. Sebastian's gaze shot to the rock, but it was still surrounded, shades flying in rhythmic circles as a black column of shadow encased the stone, swirling and moving skyward, just as it had the night Sebastian first saw the shades doing their dance.

"Now, James," Parker yelled as William thrashed and the

attacking shades scratched Parker, pulling at him and trying to free the possessed person he held.

James conjured a ball of light, and the William-shade screamed. James thrust the glowing orb forward, hitting William's face. He closed his unnaturally black eyes before the light made contact. James reacted swiftly, forcing the light into his mouth instead.

Too late, William clamped his lips shut, trapping the light inside.

A shade bit Sebastian's shoulder, distracting him with sharp pain. He sent sparks into its face and it ignited, nearly burning Sebastian's hoodie along with it.

Another shade latched on to James's back. Sebastian sent fire at it, and it burst into shadow. William struggled in Parker's hold, but Parker didn't lose his grip. He grunted with effort and most likely pain as blood slid down his arms, more cuts opening as shades clawed him.

Sebastian attempted to banish the shades attacking Parker, but they kept darting out of the way. James said the words to increase the strength of his light spell and an earsplitting yell stopped Sebastian in his tracks. William went rigid as blinding light shone from his open black eyes and tightly sealed lips.

Dark shadow erupted from his skin. Parker released William, who slumped forward. The shade that had been inside him didn't dissipate. It solidified into an opaque, inky beast that seemed to swallow the daylight around it.

James banished a shade about to bite Parker in the neck. Two more lunged toward James, but before Sebastian could react, his head throbbed and his vision blurred. It hurt more than it ever had and he wasn't even using the veins' magic.

Why was it worse now? Did it mean something was changing in the veins, or was everything finally catching up with his body? Was it because the shades seemed to be doing their dance to bring back the darkness?

Sebastian swore the earth shook beneath his feet.

When his vision cleared, the pain subsiding somewhat, Sebastian found James and Parker breathing heavily, the shades attacking them gone.

"Let's get out of here," Parker panted.

James grabbed Parker's arm. "We can't leave William lying in the road."

Parker grunted and stooped to pick up the unconscious man. He'd been possessed, but Sebastian still suspected most of William's recent actions were his own. He didn't think the shade had rounded up that mob, especially not when it had said it didn't want Sebastian at Storm House. Still, they couldn't leave him lying there.

"The shades," Sebastian rasped, his voice weak. He pointed at the stone and the growing shadow surrounding it. They had to stop them before the darkness came back, except Sebastian felt like he had no energy left.

A thunderous boom cut through the air and the shades circling the stone were thrown back, blasted all the way into the surrounding buildings. The ground vibrated. Sebastian had no idea what was happening. The stabbing pain in his head stole his attention, his awareness of his surroundings going in and out. He managed to focus in time to see the black shadow clinging to the stone release its hold and spill haphazardly onto the grass.

Across the circle, a shriek sounded, making Sebastian wince in pain. He took a deep breath and pushed through it. When his focus returned, he found James staring ahead. Sebastian followed his gaze and his stomach dropped out.

The large stag that had been shot in the head and chest rose from the road. It threw its head back and screamed, then lowered it, a single onyx eye fixed on James, the other nothing but a bloody mess.

The stag charged.

James lurched out of its path, grabbing Sebastian. They stumbled. The stag corrected its course, head down and antlers pointing forward. In a matter of seconds, it would run them through.

There wasn't time to think, let alone run or try to banish the shade. Not when the animal was already dead. Sebastian did the only thing he could. He called the power of the veins to him and unleashed scalding blue power on the stag.

The blow hit the beast in the head, blasting it back as the shade was expelled from its body and destroyed. The stag slumped to the ground and the earth shook.

Sebastian dropped to his knees. Power still crackled at his fingers.

The earth trembled again like an earthquake. James wrapped his arms around Sebastian, trying to pull him up. They had to go before another dead stag rose, but Sebastian couldn't move.

The ground shook harder. The shades thrown from the stone shrieked and fled toward the forest. Then everything went black.

SEBASTIAN'S HEAD throbbed and filled his world with agony. The only thing he could concentrate on other than the pain was his breathing. He tried to use it to relax, taking steady, deep breaths.

He must have lost consciousness again, and when he was next alert, the pain wasn't so bad. Sebastian opened his eyes to a darkened room. He was at the duplex. A light lit the stairwell, so his bedroom wasn't pitch black, but he was relieved the overhead light wasn't on.

"James?" he croaked, throat dry.

"I'm here, sweetheart." James lay next to him, an arm around Sebastian. He propped himself up and filled Sebastian's vision.

Tears welled in Sebastian's eyes. "I'm sorry."

"There's no need to be. You saved us. That's nothing to be

sorry for." James stroked Sebastian's forehead. "Can I get you anything?"

"My head," was all Sebastian could manage.

James hurried from the bed and returned with water and a pill. Sebastian accepted gratefully. James passed him some nuts and an apple, and Sebastian forced them down. He knew he needed food but everything was so uncomfortable that eating didn't feel as satisfying as it usually did after magic use.

The duplex shook.

Sebastian set the apple aside, directing a wide-eyed stare at James.

He grimaced. "Yeah, that keeps happening."

Sebastian remembered the earth shaking before he passed out. "It's not a normal earthquake, is it?"

"No." James rubbed Sebastian's back. "The tremors are strongest closest to the veins, and Parker said they're even worse at the vein intersection."

"He went out to Storm House?"

James nodded. "He and Hazel took one of the fuel cells while Eli and Eleanor stayed in town. They connected it to the veins just like we did, but it doesn't seem to have had any impact."

Sebastian tried to absorb James's words. "You gave them the transfer spell to use?"

"Yeah. They returned it after. Everyone's at Parker's, but I thought it might be best if we stayed here. At least until you were awake."

"How long have I been out?" The night sky gave Sebastian a sudden jolt. "The shades tried to bring back the darkness, but they failed. Right?"

James nodded. "It's almost ten p.m. That's nothing but a normal night sky outside." The building shook again. James paused before saying, "The veins must not have been stable enough to hold the shades' darkness spell this time. Their attempt to use the veins again seems to have caused the tremors."

"Think it means things are close to exploding?" Sebastian whispered.

"Yeah," James replied, voice low and fear in his eyes. "Most people have evacuated. Other than the ones who can't."

Sebastian grabbed James's hand and squeezed. He let the reality of the situation sink in. They were at the end. They'd run out of time.

There was only one thing left to try.

Sebastian's heart pounded. "We have to go to Storm House."

Alarm flashed across James's face as if he knew exactly what Sebastian was thinking. "No. Why would we go out there? We don't have any way of fixing this."

"Sacrifice is how magic works in the world of blood and bone," Sebastian repeated the shade's words. It had been right. Even the personal energy cost of casting spells could be considered a small sacrifice. "What if I was right about putting everything back together with me as the missing piece? That shade said it wouldn't let me bar them from this world, so I must be able to do something."

James shook his head desperately, and Sebastian felt immensely sad, like he'd fallen into a pit that had no bottom. James's eyes shone. Sebastian wanted to take his pain away but didn't know if he could, and that scared him.

Sebastian forced himself to remain as calm as he could. "Correcting the imbalance and closing the gateway would bar them from Moonlight Falls."

"But this isn't how it ends," James pleaded, tears breaking free and falling down his cheeks.

Sebastian wiped them away, leaning in to brush a soft kiss against James's lips. "It'd be better than waiting for the explosion. This way, not everyone has to die."

James choked on a sob. "You really think *this* is what we have to do?"

Sebastian nodded, unable to speak. Neither of them seemed

to be able to spell it out. It was deeply unfair, but Sebastian couldn't deny that joining the veins in place of the missing piece felt like the only solution. That shade's words hadn't been random, and Sebastian had always suspected the beasts knew more about the inner workings of the veins than humans did.

"Okay." James gripped Sebastian's hand, his expression hardening. "I'm coming with you."

"What?" Sebastian jerked back. "You can't, James. I can't make you watch as I…"

"Who said I'd watch. I'm *coming with you*." James took hold of either side of Sebastian's face in a tender but firm grip. "I'm not leaving you. We're in this together no matter what that means, sweetheart. I'll go with you wherever you need me. There isn't anything I won't face for you."

Sebastian's throat clogged and he blinked away tears at the pure love in James's expression. "Even death?"

"Even that." James sounded calm in a way Sebastian found hard to believe. Was James really offering to walk into the veins with him, to go into the earth? Sebastian couldn't accept that.

James pulled Sebastian against his chest, crushing them together. "I've been afraid of death my whole life, but I'm not anymore. Not when it means standing by you and supporting you. Not when it means doing everything I can for you."

"James, that doesn't make sense," Sebastian sobbed as the duplex gave a violent shake and something crashed off the counter in the bathroom.

"It doesn't have to make sense." James kissed the top of Sebastian's head. "You just have to know I love you, and I'm here for you. Come on, let's go save the town."

SEBASTIAN

SEBASTIAN LET James drive him out to Storm House. The ground shook beneath them the whole way, the tremors sending painful jolts along Sebastian's already frayed nerves. He had to talk James out of coming with him. This last-ditch effort to save Moonlight Falls was something only Sebastian could do because of the curse passed down in his blood. It wasn't for James or anyone else who had been trapped to bear.

As they pulled up to the Storm House gate, the tremors worsened. The whole truck shook and James braced himself in his seat.

"Are you sure about this, James?" Sebastian asked.

James looked at him with sad determination. "Yes, I'm coming with you."

"But why? If this works and stops the explosion, you don't have to die."

James bit his lip, his resolve faltering. "Do you really think you have to die?"

Sebastian gave a helpless shrug. "How else will I return to the veins and fill in for the missing piece? I don't think I can survive that." Sebastian imagined stepping into the strange hole at the vein intersection. He'd either become part of the veins or fall through the portal to Beyond. Survival didn't seem likely in either case. Beyond wasn't for the living, after all.

"No, I don't think you'll survive going into the veins," James agreed, like speaking the words hurt him.

Sebastian covered James's hand with his. "Then stay here."

James pulled away and unbuckled his seatbelt. "What if that humanoid shade is there and tries to stop you? You might need me."

Sebastian hadn't thought of that. He didn't know what to do. This already hurt too much. He was going to lose everything and James sharing his fate was worse than anything. "I appreciate what you're doing for me, but I promise I won't think you've abandoned me if you stay outside the gates. I know you choose me, James. I'm yours, and nothing will change that."

James got out of the truck without replying and walked around to Sebastian's door. He opened it and held out a hand, expression anguished but resolute.

Sebastian slipped his hand into James's. "You know I don't want this, right?"

James squeezed his fingers. "I know, sweetheart. I don't want it either, but you wouldn't be you if you waited for the explosion and didn't try to save everyone any way you could. You're good, Sebastian. You're selfless and caring even when the world hasn't been kind to you." James pulled Sebastian from the truck and closed the door. "You're amazing."

"I don't know," Sebastian mumbled.

"I do." James smiled softly. "You deserve the best in life, Sebastian. I just wish I'd had time to give it to you."

"You did." Sebastian clung to James, hoping he could tell how deeply Sebastian meant it.

James squeezed him harder. "Not nearly enough."

Sebastian had to agree with that. But he couldn't dwell on it, or he might lose his nerve. "Do you think I'm right? This afternoon, you were adamant I was wrong about this, that I wasn't truly part of the veins enough to make this work."

James gritted his teeth. "What the shade said while possessing William made me less sure, and I understand you're trying to solve this with everything you have, even if I wish you wouldn't. But don't get me wrong, if I didn't think we were going to die soon regardless, I'd never let you do this."

The ground beneath their feet shook so violently that Sebastian and James were thrown against the truck.

For some reason, James's changed opinion made Sebastian less sure about this sacrifice. He could be wrong. He was throwing his life away based on nothing but a depressing vision, his own wild conjectures, and a vicious shade's words. But Sebastian knew he was dead either way. The explosion was coming, and James was right. He had to try to save the people he could.

He could do this and figure out a way to make James let him go. He had to be able to save James too.

The gate was unlocked. Parker must not have bothered with the chain and padlock when he and Hazel had left earlier. Sebastian and James were unsteady on their feet as they walked up the driveway. The shaking didn't let up and Sebastian was surprised to see Storm House still standing.

Nervous chills spread out over Sebastian's body as they went. The property was suspiciously free of shades. He'd expected there to be hordes of the beasts. Did they know destruction was near? Had they given up on Moonlight Falls now that their gateway was about to explode?

James held Sebastian's hand tight as they passed the cemetery and entered the trees. Wood creaked and the wind howled. The walk through the woods didn't seem real. Sebastian was detached from everything around him, almost convinced he wasn't going to die even though it was what he intended. He had James at his side, and that made him believe things would be all right, even now.

As they approached the clearing, an eerie glow shone through the trees. Cool throbbing light danced along the dirt and reflected off the trees. Sebastian's head ached, the pain undulating with the strange light display.

"Do you want to keep going?" James asked in his ear.

Sebastian hadn't realized they'd stopped walking. There was so much motion between the ground shaking, light flashing, and the spinning sensation in his head.

"I think my headaches are connected to what's happening to the veins." Sebastian rubbed his temple. "We need to keep going. The increased pain could mean I'm right about being connected enough for this to work."

James helped Sebastian along. "Or it could just be the aftereffects of using the veins."

"I know. There won't be any proving me right or wrong before I do this." A deeper sense of doubt washed over Sebastian. He wanted to save James and Moonlight Falls, but what if he couldn't? What if sacrificing himself was throwing away his last moments with James before everything blew up anyway? What if James was determined to jump off this cliff with him and there was no saving him?

Sebastian stepped past the trees into the clearing. The hole was wide and dark, except for the eerie light glowing at the edge of the void. The ground shook, causing the light to vibrate and pulse. The hole widened.

Fear and doubt ate at Sebastian. "What if I'm wrong? What if I go in there and die, and nothing happens?"

James gripped Sebastian's shoulders. "You might be wrong. You don't have to do this."

Sebastian shivered. He hadn't expected this to be easy, yet he hadn't been prepared for the tightness gripping his chest or the bone-deep urge he had to run away. He didn't know what to do. If he was too afraid to try, he'd be dooming Eli, Hazel, Parker, and Eleanor all to die along with James. Judging by the mess of otherworldly magic before him, there was no doubt the explosion was coming.

James's grip on Sebastian tightened. "I'll help you do this if it's what you want. I'll go with you, Sebastian. But we don't have to. We could be wrong. There could still be another way."

"How?" Tears filled Sebastian's eyes and his head ached like someone was squeezing his brain. "Sacrifice is how magic works in the world of blood and bone."

"Blood and bone," James mumbled, frowning deeply for a long moment. Then his eyes widened. "Sebastian!" James shook him. "*Blood and bone.*"

"Yeah, so?" Sebastian had no idea what James was getting at. Confusion pushed away some of the sadness threatening to consume him. "What about it?"

"You can make a sacrifice of blood and bone." James let out a hysterical laugh. "You don't need to die. Why do *you* have to return to the veins? Blood-and-bone magic almost never requires all of a person. What if your blood and bone are enough to return the missing piece to the veins?"

Sebastian blinked. The earth jolted, throwing him against James's chest.

They clung to each other, James seeming to vibrate as he spoke. "We already figured out that the curse and imbalance weren't about life. Life sacrifice shouldn't be the solution. Why can't you make the system whole with just a piece of you?"

"I don't know. You're right. That could work. We can at least try it. Fuck, James. If this is it and it's not the end..." Sebastian sobbed as hope, even more painful than the despair he'd just pushed away, swelled inside him.

"This isn't the end, Sebastian." James pressed a kiss to his lips. "You were made a part of this through blood and bone, and you'll put it all back together the same way. A piece of you for the missing piece. I know this is it. I can feel it."

"How am I going to do this?" Sebastian's stomach turned.

Blood was easy enough, but bone… "I guess I can cut off the tip of a finger."

James let out a pained whining sound. "Sebastian."

"I know." Sebastian tightened his grip on James, who held Sebastian through another intense rocking of the earth. They didn't have much time.

"I'm sorry, sweetheart, this still isn't going to be easy."

Sebastian pulled back, looking down at James. "Cutting off a finger is going to be easier than dying," he said, summoning strength he wasn't sure he actually possessed.

James grimaced. "I wouldn't say any of this is easy."

Sebastian knew that but was trying not to think about it. "Come on." He pulled James back through the trees. "We need an axe or something."

Walking through the woods was even more surreal this time. Sebastian was overwhelmed with relief and a growing dread. He'd imagined jumping into the vein intersection to be painless— whether that was true or not—but this wouldn't be. He tried to detach himself from the situation completely. He couldn't think about what a blood-and-bone sacrifice meant. Instead, he focused on the fact that James wasn't walking unnecessarily to his death.

James had saved Sebastian again. Saved him from making a colossal mistake when they still had one last thing to try, and Sebastian was beyond grateful.

Maybe the world wasn't completely unfair and Sebastian wasn't doomed. He was still so used to feeling unworthy that he'd let it cloud his judgment. It had made accepting his doomed fate feel right when it wasn't.

Sebastian was destined for good things. He was a fighter. He'd fought for himself most of his life and wasn't stopping now. Not when he and James had a whole future to spend together.

In the barn, Sebastian grabbed a hatchet. Behind him, James made a strangled sound.

"Let's not stop to think." Sebastian turned on his heel and exited the barn in a hurry.

James hastened after. "Okay, but we have to be careful how we do this." James took hold of Sebastian's hand like he couldn't stand being parted. "If you lose too much blood, we'll be in trouble."

Sebastian's stomach twisted and a helpless whimper escaped him.

"It'll be all right. I'll look after you," James murmured soothingly. The ground lurched beneath their feet, doing its best to contradict him.

Sebastian focused on the love and admiration in James's eyes and steeled himself. "I think we're running out of time."

James nodded, and they hurried back the way they'd come.

The clearing was brighter, the sickening lights pulsing more rapidly. The hole was a deep, impenetrable black that seemed to flicker and contract at the center, the motions rippling through the ground, shaking the forest.

"Think this is what it looked like when Sullivan and Nelson created the imbalance?" James asked.

"Maybe." Sebastian had to squint against the flashing lights, which weren't helping his headache. He tore his eyes away and focused on the man he loved. "Thank you for being here with me."

James smiled so delicately that Sebastian's heart cracked. "Of course, Sebastian. I'll do anything for you."

Fuck if they weren't putting that to the test.

"How are we going to do this?" Sebastian asked nervously.

James held his hand out for the hatchet.

Sebastian hesitated. "I'm not asking you to cut off my finger. I can do it. I just… What about the bleeding?"

James took the hatchet from Sebastian. "I'll have to cauterize the wound. We're too far from medical help, and the spell I used to stop your bleeding during the unbinding ritual won't work on an injury like this." James swallowed. "If I heat the hatchet with magically enhanced fire, I can use the hot metal to stop the bleeding."

Sebastian wished he hadn't eaten that half an apple. "Okay. Once that's done, we'll give my finger to the veins, and hopefully, it will put everything right."

Fear flashed across James's face. "It's a plan. Let me try and sterilize this first." He conjured a floating ball of flame, a more costly spell than conjuring sparks. James ran the blade of the hatchet through it. It was the best they could do under the circumstances.

Sebastian figured infection was a worry for another day. If they lived that long.

James let the flame go out and handed the hatchet back to Sebastian. "You should brace against a tree or a rock or something."

Sebastian spotted a fallen tree not far away, just beyond the edge of the clearing. He knelt and pressed his nondominant hand to it, curling all his fingers out of the way except for his pinky. "Fuck this is going to hurt."

"Wait!" James knelt beside him and performed the spell they used on Miss Moo to numb her skin when they'd tried to transfer the curse to her. "It won't be enough, but it's better than nothing."

Sebastian examined the hatchet. The blade was sharp, unlike the axe he used to chop firewood. Movement in the clearing caught his eye, his gaze torn from the hatchet and drawn to the center of the hole. The darkness seemed to be undulating, almost like the ocean, causing the earth to move in a way that made Sebastian seasick.

He had to do this now. "Ready, James?"

"I've got you, sweetheart."

Sebastian raised the hatchet. He didn't let himself think beyond aiming. He lined the blade up with his finger, then pulled back and swung down with all his strength. Sebastian watched the blade strike and his finger fell away. He was frozen in disbelief even though he'd meant to do it. Everything around him went silent, the pain hitting him like nothing he'd ever experienced.

Sebastian screamed, dropping the hatchet, and pulled his injured hand against his chest, cradling it with his other. He clamped his eyes shut as nausea threatened and pain almost stole his consciousness.

A firm pressure against Sebastian's back helped him hold on, but the pain was too blinding for him to think. Something clamped down on his wrist, and Sebastian thrashed before he remembered it was James and allowed his injured hand to be pulled from where he had it tucked against himself.

There was a sudden heat and his pain intensified. Shit, this was so much worse. Sebastian screamed again, trying to jerk away on instinct, but James held him tight, his chest braced against Sebastian's back and his arms around him.

The smell of burning flesh made Sebastian gag. Just when he thought he couldn't take it, it stopped.

Sebastian's cheeks were soaked and sobs shook him from head to toe. James didn't release his hold. He rocked Sebastian back and forth, murmuring in his ear. Everything hurt unbearably. Sebastian wasn't sure how he was supposed to keep functioning.

Eventually, Sebastian's head cleared enough for him to process what James was saying.

"I love you, Sebastian. I've got you. You're so brave. You're perfect. I'll never let you go." He went on and on in a stream of comfort until Sebastian stopped trembling.

"Let's finish this," Sebastian rasped. "Where did it go?" He looked down at his bloody hand to where his pinky ended at the second knuckle. It didn't seem to be bleeding anymore but looked absolutely ghastly.

"Here." James handed him his severed finger.

Sebastian took it in his uninjured hand. "Help me up?"

James hoisted Sebastian to his feet and guided him around the fallen tree and into the clearing. The ground shook so violently that he might have needed the help even if he hadn't felt like he was about to pass out.

"Oh shit." James's worried voice captured Sebastian's frayed attention.

At the center of the hole, the ripples had gotten larger, and from their tumultuous depths came a stream of shades. Beasts flew out of the gateway by the hundreds, shooting into the night sky.

Sebastian staggered forward, supported by James. The shades didn't seem to notice them. Were they trying to escape before the veins exploded and the gateway closed?

James guided Sebastian to the glowing edge of the hole. The pulsing light sent the pain in his head and hand throbbing. Sebastian clung to consciousness. He gripped James with his uninjured hand as best he could and tossed his finger into the hole with the other.

"Fucking blood and bone," he grumbled as he watched it fall.

The finger hit the roiling darkness. Even though it seemed like the surface of a churning sea, the finger didn't disappear like it would have had it been liquid. Sebastian could see his finger falling into the void. It went down and down until it disappeared in a flash of blue light.

The shaking earth went abruptly still. Sebastian let out a gasp of shock and relief.

"Look." James pointed at the glowing edge of the hole in front of them. It receded, replaced by an undisturbed forest floor as the hole continued to shrink.

"It worked," Sebastian breathed, fresh tears streaming down his cheeks.

The shades continued to fly out of the center of the hole, but it was just a dark void and no longer rippling. As the hole shrank slowly, the pulsing light lessened. Everything seemed to calm.

Then it stopped. The hole had shrunk by about a quarter, but after a minute of no progress, it didn't seem to be closing any farther.

Sebastian's heart sank and he slumped against James, letting out a sound of pain and fear. "It didn't work."

"It did." James held him tight. "The earth stopped shaking. Everything is calm."

"But the hole is still here." Sweat broke out on Sebastian's forehead. "Does that mean I have to sacrifice all of myself if a piece of me wasn't enough?" He let out an angry laugh. "A piece of the missing piece wasn't enough. How many pieces of pieces do we need? I can't cut myself up into tiny bits." Everything was cruel and funny in a way that made him want to hurl.

"Wait." James spun Sebastian around so they were facing each other. If he'd let go, Sebastian would have fallen like a felled tree. "Wait," James repeated, his eyes wild like he was panicking or thinking too fast for his brain to process. "Pieces of pieces…"

Great, James was losing his grip too.

A shriek cut across the quiet clearing. Sebastian hadn't even realized the howling wind had stopped until now.

The shades had noticed them, probably wondering what had caused the change in the veins. No more streamed in through the gateway, but a large group hovered in the clearing, all eyes focused on Sebastian and James.

"What are they waiting for?" James whispered.

In unison, all the shades cocked their heads. They paused, then straightened and shot off into the sky.

Where were they going? Sebastian hoped everyone in town was all right.

Before he could say anything, a dark figure appeared across the clearing. The large humanoid shade stood at the edge of the hole, lit by the faint glowing light.

"Leave," the otherworldly voice commanded.

That wasn't happening. Sebastian had no patience left. He was in pain and filled with dread because it looked like he'd have to sacrifice himself after all.

Should he just throw himself into the hole now, shade be damned? No, that would leave James at risk. He couldn't have that. James was going to survive this. That was all Sebastian cared about.

He pulled the power of the veins to him. It came easily, whether from practice or because he was at the intersection, he didn't know. Sebastian didn't hesitate or give the shade a chance. He pulled power out of the earth and directed it at the being, holding nothing back.

The shade lifted into the air, and for a second, Sebastian thought it was flying toward him. But no. Blue energy poured from Sebastian into the beast, holding it suspended above the hole as overwhelming power ran through Sebastian, its strength almost unfathomable.

The shade screamed and disappeared in a flash of light, the eerie yell echoing around them.

Sebastian's vision blacked out. He was ready to give in to all the pain and just have it be over. "Throw me in," he muttered.

"No." James's response was harsh in his ear.

Sebastian breathed until his vision cleared. "We don't have much time. That thing might come back any minute. I don't know how long it takes to get through the gateway. I have to close it."

"We will close it." James lowered Sebastian to the ground and propped him against a tree. "But you've already made your sacrifice. Going into the veins to die won't help."

Sebastian watched James walk over to the two fuel cells at the edge of the clearing, too pained and overwhelmed to move. "Why won't it help?"

"Because you aren't the only missing piece."

22

JAMES

JAMES COULD SEE it all so clearly it was almost frightening. His heart had broken when Sebastian had decided to sacrifice himself, and his soul had fractured to see him in so much pain, cutting off his own finger, but James was sure he'd finally figured it out.

"I don't know what you're saying, James," Sebastian pleaded from the forest floor. James felt horrible for dumping him there, but there wasn't time to stay by Sebastian's side. He had to prove he was right.

The veins had calmed. However, James wasn't sure if they'd fended off the explosion permanently or if the tremors would return. They had to finish this and do it before that shade came back. Sebastian couldn't keep using the veins to save them.

"You aren't the only missing piece," James repeated. He cast a spell to levitate the fuel cell he and Sebastian had connected to the veins, sending it into the clearing and over the glowing edge of the hole.

"Wait," Sebastian called weakly.

"The fuel cell is a stand-in for the missing piece too." James sent it to the center of the hole. "You made it one when we transferred the curse from you to it. It has the same connection to the veins you do. Watch."

James released his spell and the fuel cell fell into the void. It tumbled until it was consumed in a flash of blue light, just like Sebastian's finger.

Sebastian gasped.

James was at his side. "See." He helped Sebastian stand, and together, they watched the hole shrink.

"It's still not closing all the way," Sebastian groaned in despair, burying his face in James's neck as tremors shook his body.

The hole was smaller than before, but maybe only by another eighth, and it didn't look to be closing any farther. "We haven't put all the pieces back," James said as soothingly as he could, given the circumstances. He ran a blood-flecked hand through Sebastian's hair. "There's three more to go."

Sebastian raised his head, eyes wide. "You mean Sullivan, Simon, and Uncle Stephen?"

James nodded grimly. "Selma's spell made you all stand-ins for the missing piece of the veins. It doesn't seem like death released anyone from their connection. I'd wondered if it had—if your predecessors could have left the property after death to be buried in town—but I'd wager they couldn't have. The veins aren't about life and death. The three Storms who came before you are still a part of the veins. They might not have been able to lend more energy to the imbalance after death, but nothing has released them from being part of it all."

Sebastian, who was already frighteningly pale, went paler. "A blood-and-bone connection. Meaning we have to get blood and bone from each of them to finish this."

"I'm sorry." James cupped Sebastian's cheek.

Sebastian gave him a half-smile. "Don't be sorry, James. You're brilliant. You figured this out. I'm not the only piece. I never would have guessed that." Sebastian braced against James to stand up straighter. "Besides, I can't really say that digging up my dead relatives will be the worst part of the night. I cut off my own fucking finger."

James pulled Sebastian into a quick kiss. He couldn't help himself. Sebastian was so brave that not even this night had beaten him down. "How are you doing? I wish I could do more for how much pain you must be in."

Sebastian grimaced. "How about we head to the hospital once this is all done? Seeing as the imbalance should be restored and we shouldn't be trapped anymore."

"Good plan." James led Sebastian back through the trees. He didn't want to linger by the hole. Things may be calm, and the imminent explosion might have been stopped, but a shitload of shades had just come through the gateway, and James wasn't going to assume they wouldn't come back. It didn't seem like the beasts were giving up on their plan to take over Moonlight Falls. James just hoped they had time to dig up three graves before they were attacked again.

In the barn, James piled shovels and a hoe into a wooden cart. Sebastian seemed to regain a bit of his strength and James was beyond impressed. He didn't know if he would still be standing.

"I can't believe there's more than one piece," Sebastian said as they reached the cemetery.

"Some blood-and-bone magic is irreversible." James dumped the shovels on the ground and picked up the hoe. "Eli hinted at it when he said he didn't think that you could ever truly transfer the curse from yourself and could only pass it on through the transfer the way you'd pass it on to any blood relative. Once the curse made you a part of the veins, there was no undoing it."

"That's what I was afraid of," Sebastian whispered.

James gripped his shoulder. "I know, but that doesn't mean you can't be free. You would have always been part of the veins, *but* you returned your blood and bone to them, and once we put all the missing pieces back, the original void in the veins that Sullivan and Nelson created will be filled, releasing you all."

James found Sullivan's headstone and brought the hoe down on the earth. "Apologies," he muttered to the dead man.

"It's too bad Sullivan never figured this out," Sebastian mused. "The Storms could have avoided all of this."

James worked at loosening the topsoil. "Selma must have thought it was impossible. It doesn't seem like anyone realized her spell linked you all to the veins so completely."

"Yeah." Sebastian picked up a shovel, stabbed it into the earth, and leaned against it. "I don't think Sullivan or anyone else knew they could harness the veins as I've been doing. They didn't realize the connection went both ways and that we really were part of the vein system. If they had, they might have figured out they could put it all back together."

James hacked at the earth in silence for a few minutes before swapping the hoe for a shovel.

"I should help," Sebastian said from where he watched.

James glanced over at him. "You don't have to. These are your relatives. I imagine it would be hard to disturb them like this."

"Can't be easy for you either."

James grunted. "I'm trying not to think about it."

Sebastian made an understanding sound. "Same."

James scooped piles of earth onto the ground in front of Selma's headstone, which sat beside Sullivan's. Sebastian brought his shovel next to James and dug it into the earth. He let out a yelp of pain.

James paused his digging. "Are you okay?"

Sebastian shook out his hand. "My finger. Ow, shit, that hurts."

"You don't have to help. It's probably not good to get the wound all dirty."

Sebastian whipped off his hoodie, then his shirt. With the hoodie back on his body, he ripped his shirt and wrapped a strip around the hand missing its pinky, covering the injury. "Better than nothing."

"Suppose that's true." James got back to digging, starting to worry this would take too long. He wanted to insist Sebastian rest, but he probably needed any help he could get.

Sebastian cast a spell to help soften the earth before picking his shovel back up, but even then, it wasn't easy digging.

James lost himself in his aching muscles and the sweat breaking out on his back and neck. Sebastian sat back to rest frequently, but neither of them spoke. It was grim work. The only thing keeping it from being too disturbing was probably the fact that they'd both thought self-sacrifice was on the table not long ago. Compared to that, James would take anything.

It felt like a miracle to have Sebastian at his side, the earth no longer trembling, doom pushed back and out of sight. James was relieved and hopeful but still frightened. They weren't finished yet, and getting there looked like it would scar him for life.

His shovel hit something hard. He scraped the dirt, revealing a dark-colored coffin. A chill traveled down James's spine as he carefully removed the last of the dirt from around it.

Sebastian frowned at the casket from where he was perched at the edge of the grave. "I don't think I can be in denial about what we're doing any longer."

"I'm sorry." James squeezed his knee. "None of them deserve to be disrespected like this."

"No, but I think they'd want us to do this if they knew it would correct the imbalance and end the curse."

"Of course they would." James climbed out of the grave. He used his levitation spell to lift the coffin from the earth and place it in the cart. "Two more to go."

Sebastian followed him to Simon's grave. "We aren't opening them up, right?"

James suppressed a shiver. "No. I don't think I could. We'll have to return them to the veins in their coffins."

Sebastian nodded and handed James the hoe.

Digging graves took forever, even with magic. Moving all the soil out of the way with a spell would have been too costly, but by the time they were halfway done with Stephen's grave, James was considering it, draining himself be damned.

He was sick with exhaustion, his clothes soaked with sweat. He had no idea what time it was. The only positive he could cling to was that the shades had stayed away.

Sebastian let out a choked sob.

James rested a dirty hand on the small of Sebastian's back. He didn't ask if Sebastian was okay. Of course he wasn't, and James didn't want to imply he should be. "What is it, sweetheart?"

"I'm just so angry," Sebastian choked out. "And sad. What happened to Stephen—abandoned here except for me visiting—was horrible. He died so young, only fifty-three. It had to be the isolation. He should have had a better life." Sebastian wiped his eyes and met James's gaze. "I feel guilty for giving him a hard time growing up and for how mad I was at him when he died and left me here. It wasn't his fault, but I focused my anger on him. I wish I hadn't. I wish my final conversation with him had gone differently."

James wrapped his arms around Sebastian. "I'm sure he understood your reaction to learning about the curse. One final conversation doesn't erase all the years you had together. You loved him, and he knew that."

"I hassled him about not leaving the house," Sebastian admitted in a pained voice.

"He knew you didn't know better. You're a kind person, Sebastian. Stephen knew that. I'm sure he was glad to have you in his life."

Sebastian sniffed. "I just hate this. I hate having to throw him in a creepy supernatural hole after everything."

James stroked Sebastian's hair. "At least it can't hurt him now. And he'd want you to be free. You said it yourself."

Sebastian pulled away and picked up his shovel. "You're right.

We have to keep going." He tossed a scoop of dirt to the side, letting out a ragged breath. "Saying all that aloud helped."

"I'm glad." James clapped Sebastian on the shoulder and got back to digging.

Tears ran down Sebastian's cheeks as James levitated Stephen's coffin out of his grave. James held Sebastian's hand, hoping it was at least somewhat comforting. He wished Sebastian didn't have to go through this. If there was a way to save him this anguish, James would have.

At least they were almost there. The end was in sight. Once they got through this, they could relax and process this whole horrible night, and they'd have all the time in the world to heal from it.

James and Sebastian pulled the cart along the forest path. James used more magic to steady the coffins. He didn't think he'd be able to keep going if one fell and burst open, leaving the occupant well and truly disturbed from their final resting place.

In the clearing, James was relieved to see the hole just as they'd left it. The edges shimmered but it was otherwise still. The earth hadn't shaken once since Sebastian offered his finger to the veins.

"Who would you like to say goodbye to first?" James asked.

Sebastian put a hand on his uncle's coffin. "Stephen."

James levitated the casket to the ground and set it on the edge of the hole.

Sebastian gazed down at it, taking James's hand. "Goodbye, Stephen. I'm sorry things couldn't be different. I'm sorry I blamed you even though you were as much a victim of this as I was. I hope you've been free of everything the curse made you endure over the last six years and that death has given you what life couldn't. I love you and will always remember you. You were a parent to me and helped me as much as you could. I forgive you for giving me this curse over my sister, and when I look back, I'll try to remember the good instead of the lies. Letting me do this to you" —Sebastian gestured to the hole— "will allow me to have a future and time to look back on my life with you. So thank you." Sebastian cut a sidelong look at James, eyes glassy with unshed tears. "Help me push?"

James's throat thickened. He nodded, and they stooped down.

One solid push and the coffin was falling into the hole, Stephen fulfilling his destiny to return to the veins. As the coffin disappeared from sight, a flash of blue signaling Stephen's farewell, the light glowing at the edges of the opening flickered and went out.

Sebastian choked on another sob and then cleared his throat. He stood. "No more speeches. I can't take much more of this."

James leaned in close and kissed him on the cheek. "You're doing great. We're almost there." The hole was even smaller now, almost half of what it had been when they'd arrived that night.

James levitated the next coffin down. It landed in the dirt with a thud. James braced his hands on his knees, taking a deep breath.

"Are you okay?" Sebastian placed a delicate hand on James's back.

"Fine. Just doing a lot of magic." He straightened. "I'll be able to rest soon. Let's lift the last one down now."

In unison, they turned toward Sullivan's coffin sitting in the cart. James froze. A shade hovered above it, head cocked. It seemed their time had run out.

23

SEBASTIAN

Irritation flared in Sebastian's chest. He was so damn sick of shades.

The night had been too much, and saying goodbye to Stephen like that had been harder than he could have prepared for.

Sebastian wanted this done. Now.

He shot sparks at the shade and it burst into flames. Without hesitating, he stooped to push the next coffin into the veins. "Rest easy, Simon."

The coffin fell away.

Out of nowhere, something swiped at Sebastian's legs and knocked him off his feet. He was yanked backward by the ankle as the edge of the hole receded, closing farther. He scrambled in the dirt, trying to stop himself as he was dragged into the trees. He couldn't get enough leverage to flip over and his hand hurt even worse than before, making it impossible to grab ahold of anything for long.

"*James!*" Sebastian shouted but got no answer. *Shit! Where was he?*

Sebastian was dragged deeper into the trees, away from the clearing. His hoodie rode up, leaving his stomach and chest vulnerable to the rough forest floor. His side slammed into a tree. Sebastian grunted in pain but managed to grab the slim trunk with his uninjured arm. He pulled against whatever was dragging him, but its hold on his legs was too strong.

Sebastian managed to twist around and landed on his back, letting go of the tree. Instead of weakening his captive's grip, it seemed to do nothing. Sebastian looked down at his feet. Black tendrils wound around his legs from ankle to mid-calf.

The tendrils extended into the forest, disappearing into the dark. Most likely, the rest of the writhing mass of shadowy feelers was somewhere beyond. Sebastian didn't know if this tendril-thing was a creature or some sort of shadow magic created by intelligent shades. It seemed to be treated as expendable by the humanoid shade before, like a layer of defense, and Sebastian feared the humanoid shade was lurking somewhere in the dark.

He was hauled deeper into the woods. The tendrils holding him wound farther up his legs until they were at his knees. He shot sparks at them, desperate to escape and find James, who was nowhere in sight.

One of the sparks caught, setting fire to a tendril and causing it to scream. Sebastian let out a shout of his own, hot fire now wrapped around his leg. The burning tendril broke away from the rest of the vine-like feelers and burst into smoke, leaving Sebastian's jeans singed.

Another tendril replaced the vanquished one almost instantly.

"Fuck," Sebastian muttered. He was so tired. Everything hurt. But he was so close to finishing this, to fixing the veins and rendering his family's cure moot. He was so close to freedom.

The tendrils ceased their dragging and Sebastian lay still. Part of him didn't think he'd be able to move. He wished he could go to sleep and deal with all this when he recovered. But he couldn't let pain or exhaustion stop him. He pushed himself into a sitting position and squinted into the dark forest.

Movement in the trees beyond caught his eye, but he couldn't make anything out. He was wasting time trying to see through the shadows. Sebastian conjured a light and pushed it forward to illuminate the forest.

The mass of tendrils was only ten feet away, pulsing and writhing, hovering above the forest floor. To the right, James was bound by shadowy feelers, his arms clamped to his sides and his whole body tightly wound. A tendril wrapped around his face, gagging him. He thrashed, his eyes wild.

Rage filled Sebastian. The feelers binding his legs continued to wind up his body until he was wrapped tight to the waist. These shadowy creatures from Beyond didn't belong in this world. They weren't allowed to ruin everything for him and James when they were so close.

Close but not there yet.

Sebastian's whole body flashed cold and clammy as a horrible realization hit him. What if something happened to Sullivan's coffin while he was tied up like this? What if his remains were destroyed or stolen and he couldn't be returned to the veins?

Sebastian released a cry of fury and pain. He let all the anger and sadness he'd harbored throughout his life—and over the course of this night—come pouring out of him, giving him energy and burning like a fire in him.

Sebastian reached for the veins' power and it came like a well-trained dog. He directed it with a wave of his injured hand and cut the tendrils binding him off at the base of the writhing mass hovering before him. Sebastian didn't even hear their screams. He shot power at the mass, letting raw energy cut across the writhing shadows until it found its center and the whole thing exploded into nothing.

James dropped to the ground.

Sebastian slowly crawled toward him on all fours, his breathing heaving. He didn't think he could stand. His energy flagged as a new pain in his head threatened to steal his consciousness.

James staggered over to him. "That shade is back."

Sebastian growled. He seemed beyond speech, like he'd gone into some feral survival mode. He let his light go out, plunging them into darkness. His regular magic was almost completely depleted, but he still felt the crackle of the veins under his skin.

"I saw it over here." James helped Sebastian stand. "Fuck, I'm sorry, sweetheart. I'm useless against these beasts."

Sebastian wanted to say it was okay but couldn't form words.

James conjured a light and sent it in the direction he'd mentioned seeing the shade. There was nothing there.

"Let's get back to the clearing." James helped Sebastian along. He seemed alert, gaze scanning the dark forest around them. At least one of them was.

They were almost at the tree line when James stopped abruptly. Ahead of them, the humanoid shade stooped over the cart and the remaining coffin. The lid was open.

Sebastian's rage came back with a vengeance. He and James might have defiled his relatives' graves by digging them up, but this beast had no right to go poking around.

This shade was leaving the human world and not coming back.

Sebastian could feel the vein intersection humming in the center of the clearing like he never had before. He'd let the power go too quickly when he'd banished the humanoid shade before. Now, with the power buzzing in his body, he could feel the passage between worlds. It was faint, as if it was closing along with the hole, but it was there.

Stepping away from James, Sebastian moved out of the cover of the trees. "I thought I told you to leave."

The shade's blank face snapped up as if to fix its nonexistent gaze on Sebastian. An eerie laugh echoed in Sebastian's head.

He ignored it, instead focusing on the gateway. As one of its keepers, he found he could command it just like he commanded the raw power of the veins. Instead of sending the blue fire sparking at his fingers to banish the shade once more, Sebastian used the gateway to call anything from Beyond back to where it had come from, forcing the shifting energy between worlds to act like a magnet.

The humanoid shade staggered backward, away from the open coffin, and let out a hiss.

Something whizzed past Sebastian and flew into the hole. Another dark shape came careening in from the other side of the clearing.

"They're shades!" James exclaimed, bewildered.

More shades from the surrounding forest were sucked back into Beyond. Sebastian could feel the magnetic pull within his own body, making him dizzy. It didn't hurt like it did when he directed the veins' raw power, but the strange sensation threatened to steal his consciousness all the same.

The humanoid shade braced itself on its knees, straining against the gateway's pull as lesser shades flew past it and disappeared into the hole.

Sebastian didn't have time for this. He staggered forward, closing the coffin lid as he passed. The shade was dragged back a foot but still resisted the pull of the gateway. Sebastian took a deep breath and braced himself. He released one more blast of blue power, hitting the shade in the face. It jolted and, unable to resist the pull of the gateway any longer, was sucked backward, disappearing into the darkness of the void.

Sebastian released the veins' power, pushing it violently away from him. "The coffin," he gasped, not sure if his vision had gone or if he'd closed his eyes.

There was a scraping sound and a grunt of exertion from James. "Done."

An arm wrapped around Sebastian's waist. He leaned into James and blinked the darkness from his vision in time to see the hole shrinking. It closed until it was only about a foot across, then stopped.

James went stiff beside Sebastian. "Why isn't it closing all the way?"

Sebastian stared at the hole. He wanted to cry. They'd put all the pieces back. Four generations of Storms had held this intersection together and returning their bits of the missing piece should have been enough. What more could they give?

"What are we missing?" Sebastian whispered, his throat hoarse.

"I don't know." James began to tremble. "You made your sacrifice. There's nothing left."

"You're right. I don't think I have to give up my life for this, but we're missing something. One more connection to the veins."

"Selma?" James suggested in desperation.

Sebastian shook his head and immediately regretted it. He took a deep breath. "No, she never tied herself to this," he gritted out.

"Then what?"

Through the pain, something clicked, and Sebastian smiled. "Nelson."

JAMES

"Nᴇʟsᴏɴ!" James cried. He wanted to kick something. "We don't have his body. He ran away, escaping the consequences."

"Not entirely." Sebastian's smile was tired and his eyes were tight with pain. "Selma linked him to his brother. It must have been a link to the veins as well, and not just to Sullivan. I knew Sullivan could force Nelson to feed the imbalance but didn't realize it made him a part of this, just like the rest of us. He wasn't trapped, so I wrote him off."

Sebastian took a staggering step into the woods, away from the clearing. James hurried to help him.

"But we don't have his body," James protested.

"We don't need it. All we need is blood and bone."

It took a second for Sebastian's words to register. When they did, James wanted to laugh. "The teeth in the study."

"Damn right. That creepy shit is going to save both our asses and the town." Sebastian winced, doubling over for a moment before pushing on. "The doll has his blood on it. We have what we need."

"Thank fuck," James breathed, making Sebastian laugh feebly.

James hardly registered the walk to the house. He was

increasingly disoriented, his exhaustion playing with his mind. It felt like the night would never end.

At last he crossed the front porch and wrenched the door to Storm House open. "I'll get everything. Wait here."

"No." Sebastian gripped James's arm, his voice more steady than it had been in a while. "I have to see this through." He stepped over the threshold into Storm House. "After everything, this house doesn't scare me. I've faced worse tonight. Coming in here one last time to destroy the curse that trapped me doesn't feel like a bad thing."

James followed, gazing adoringly at the man he loved. "I'm in constant awe of you."

Sebastian blushed. "Who knew you were so easy to impress. I distinctly remember you playing hard to get."

James snorted, leading the way up the stairs. "Nothing you've accomplished has been easy, Sebastian."

He shrugged. "Maybe not. But I'm clearly willing to work for it."

James laughed. "Even at a time like this, you manage to fill me with joy."

Sebastian nudged his shoulder. "Only because you like me working for it."

"Nightmare," James muttered with deep affection.

They reached the landing and Sebastian pulled him close, bringing their lips together. "I love you."

"I love you too. Now, let's throw some creepy, eighty-year-old junk into a supernatural hole."

Sebastian smiled, his dimples brightening his face. "Whoever thinks blood-and-bone rituals have to be serious clearly hasn't met us."

"Which is a good thing. We'd probably get a lecture."

Sebastian opened Selma's room and ducked in to grab the Nelson-doll from her dressing table. James was glad Sebastian didn't seem affected by returning to this part of Storm House.

He'd conquered that fear.

They hurried to the study, James lighting an oil lamp along the way. The jar of teeth was on the shelf where they'd left it, and when he grabbed it this time, he didn't scream.

"Never thought I'd be glad to see these." The yellowing label bearing *N. Storm* and *S. Storm* gave James a sense of relief.

"I never thought I'd be glad my predecessors didn't clean out the house. Imagine if the jar had been thrown away."

James grimaced. "I'd rather not."

"No." Sebastian pulled him toward the door. "Let's go."

If they could have run to the clearing, they would have. At this point, James was glad they were both still upright and moving. He didn't think he had much magic left in him, and Sebastian had to be running purely off adrenaline.

He couldn't wait to lie down, sleep, and wake up to the rest of his life with this amazing man.

They made it across the property to find the clearing as they'd left it.

Sebastian paused next to the fuel cell Hazel and Parker had brought out earlier that night. "Are we sure this doesn't have to go in as well?"

"I don't think it does." James considered the fuel cell. "And not just because I'd like to take it back to Gray Electrical when this is over."

Sebastian raised his brows.

"This fuel cell was connected by transferring the curse from Hazel, who was trapped by the secret. None of us trapped from learning about the veins have the true connection to them that you and your relatives do."

Sebastian nodded, seeming satisfied. "Thank goodness for that. Imagine if we had to cut fingers off everyone stuck here. I really wouldn't be popular." He turned his back on the fuel cell and approached the hole.

James joined him.

Sebastian's tired eyes found James in the dim light of the oil lamp. "Together?"

"Together," James agreed, and they tossed the items into the black abyss.

The doll and jar of teeth disappeared from sight as they tumbled into the darkness. James grabbed Sebastian's hand, not tearing his eyes away.

Bright light flared, almost blinding James. He shielded his face, holding Sebastian tight as the light shot up into the sky, illuminating the forest. For a split second, it was bright as day, then they were plunged back into darkness.

Sebastian gasped and crumpled against James.

"Sweetheart?" James clutched Sebastian, swiping Sebastian's messy hair from his face to find his eyes closed. "What's wrong?"

Sebastian groaned. "I felt it." He gripped James's arm to steady himself, only to wince in pain at using his injured hand. "It was like something was just pulled out of my core."

"Like your connection to the veins was severed?"

Sebastian glanced at James, suddenly alert. "Just like that." He looked down at their feet, James following suit, finding the hole completely gone. It looked like it had never been there.

"I think we did it," Sebastian whispered.

"We did." James squeezed him and kissed his tangled curls. "*You* did it!"

"Can we lie down now?" Sebastian slumped limply against James once more, his voice weakening. "You're the only thing holding me up, and I think it's gonna be a while before I can manage it on my own."

"We need to get you to the hospital." James summoned the last of his strength—something he didn't think he possessed after the night he'd had, but he would pretend and hope that was enough—and hoisted Sebastian into his arms. Putting one foot carefully in front of the other, James walked through the woods for what was hopefully the last time.

"Can we go after I sleep?" Sebastian whined. "I think I'm going to be sick if I keep moving."

"Be sick if you have to, but I'm not putting you down in the dirt. You need a doctor."

"You take such good care of me," Sebastian mumbled.

James snorted, ignoring his protesting muscles as he walked. "Not leaving you bloody and drained in a dark forest is hardly a high standard of care."

"Whatever. Take the compliment, James. I'm tired."

"Okay, sweetheart. I promise you can rest soon."

JAMES SETTLED Sebastian into his truck's passenger seat and climbed in on the driver's side. He wouldn't be able to make it all the way to Apple Valley. He'd pass out at the wheel and kill them both, but if he could get to Parker's, someone else could take them the rest of the way.

Sebastian went quiet not long after pulling away from Storm House. He slumped in his seat, and whenever James pried his tired eyes from the road to check, Sebastian was unmoving, his eyes closed.

Even though James knew Sebastian needed rest, it worried him. He hadn't let himself worry all night, and it seemed to be catching up with him. The longer he drove, the worse his anxiety became. His hands trembled and his chest tightened until his breaths turned shallow.

James wasn't sure how he made it through the drive to town, only that he did.

He pulled up at Parker's in a sudden panic that no one would be there. What if the hordes of shades he and Sebastian had seen coming through the gateway had come to attack? What if his friends and Eli had been hurt or worse?

Before James could get a handle on his spiraling thoughts, the door to Parker's house flew open and Eli ran toward the truck. He yanked James's door open and pulled James into a hug.

"Oh my god, you're all right!" Eli cried.

Parker was a step behind him. They both looked fine.

"We need to go to the hospital," James managed to say.

Eli released him from his crushing hold, eyes wide. "Can we get to the hospital?"

"We should be able to." James turned toward Sebastian in the passenger seat. He still hadn't moved. "We need to hurry." He gripped Sebastian's hand. "Sweetheart, wake up."

Sebastian didn't respond.

Tears blurred James's vision. Sebastian had to be okay. He was probably just resting, but James couldn't control his fear that Sebastian wouldn't wake up this time.

Parker appeared at Sebastian's door, opening it and lifting Sebastian out.

"Wait," James called.

"I'll drive." Parker gave him a steady nod and took Sebastian away.

Tears fell from James's eyes. They had to get to the hospital, but he couldn't be separated from Sebastian. He didn't know what to do other than stay by his side. What if, after everything, Sebastian died?

"Come on." Eli pulled on James's arm. "Into my car."

James looked at him in confusion. "Is Sebastian okay?"

Eli exchanged words with Parker. "He's breathing. Let's go." Eli guided James to the back seat of his car as if James were a lost child. "You're probably in shock. You need the hospital too."

James collapsed into the back seat. Sebastian was there, his head lolled back against the seat. James was vaguely aware of Eli buckling him in as he reached for Sebastian. It was awkward holding him with both their seatbelts on, but James couldn't let him go.

It hadn't been too much, had it? Sebastian was going to be fine. He'd been talking and joking not long ago. True, he hadn't been able to walk to the truck, but that didn't mean anything.

Sebastian would wake up just like all the other times he'd passed out after using the veins. James tried to convince himself this was guaranteed, but he couldn't ignore the fact that Sebastian had gone through so much more than anyone should have to bear tonight.

It was the longest car ride of James's life. He didn't even register the moment Parker drove past the boundary that had trapped them. He hardly noticed the sun rising, warm and golden, except for the fact that it lit Sebastian beautifully, making him look like a fallen and battered angel.

Sebastian didn't stir the whole ride. The only sign he hadn't slipped away was his soft breaths in and out.

At last, they arrived at the hospital emergency room and James leaped from the car, only to stumble. He'd intended to carry Sebastian inside but was too unsteady on his feet to stand without bracing against the car.

Eli appeared at his side. "Let me help you."

James shook his head. "Get Sebastian."

"Parker's got Sebastian." Eli hoisted one of James's bloody and dirt-covered arms over his shoulders, propping him up.

James turned in time to see Parker carrying Sebastian through the sliding ER doors. James relaxed infinitesimally. Sebastian was going to get the care he needed. James clung to the hope it would be enough.

Inside, James was admitted and seen by nurses and a doctor. He could barely keep one moment straight from the next. He'd used too much magic, his body ached, and being unable to calm his worries was doing bad things to his blood pressure. He hated that he didn't know what was happening with Sebastian.

He was so tired. It made his brain foggy, but he couldn't have fallen asleep if he'd wanted to. James lay there in his hospital bed, sick with worry, wishing he could just get through this to what came next.

James had no idea how long it had been when Eli came bustling behind the curtain blocking James's bed from the rest of the ER. "Sebastian is awake."

Some of the tension was released from James's body. "He'll be okay?"

"Yes, James. He'll recover just fine." Eli squeezed his hand. "The doctors aren't happy about his finger though."

Tears of relief filled James's eyes. "No one's happy about that. Least of all Sebastian."

Eli gave him a searching look. "What the hell happened?"

James sank back into his pillows, having trouble focusing on his brother. "Had to put the pieces of the veins back together." He closed his eyes. Maybe he could sleep after all. "Tell you the rest later."

Sebastian was in the hospital for a week while doctors treated his burned and severed finger. They ended up amputating his pinky back to the first knuckle since cauterizing the original wound the way they did had caused significant tissue damage. Sebastian was just grateful for the painkillers.

And for James, who wouldn't leave his side.

Sebastian had been admitted to a room, and once James was released from the ER, he took up permanent residence in the chair beside Sebastian's bed. Sebastian wished James would go home and get some proper rest, but he was also warmed by his constant presence. He loved that James was there every time he opened his eyes.

At the moment, James was fast asleep, snoring, his head tilting in a way that looked less than comfortable. Sebastian was pretty sure he was drooling.

"You look happy," Dr. Reese said as she entered Sebastian's room.

Sebastian tore his eyes away from James. "I'm feeling a lot better."

"Good." She gave him a tight smile.

Sebastian had the impression Dr. Reese was displeased with him for purposely cutting off his own finger. He'd explained that it had been part of ritual magic and vital in preventing Moonlight Falls from exploding, but he wasn't entirely sure she believed him.

The secret-binding was completely gone, along with the curse. Eli had visited yesterday and told Sebastian how Eleanor had reported the incident in full to any state official who would listen and several who wouldn't, despite their brush-offs.

"You're free to go home today," Dr. Reese continued. "You'll need to book follow-up appointments to check on your healing progress, and we'd recommend hand therapy, but unless you have any further questions, the nurses have your discharge papers ready to go."

"Thank you so much." Sebastian disentangled himself from the hospital sheets. "I don't have any questions."

The doctor gave him a stern look. "Take care of yourself."

Sebastian planned to.

He quickly pulled on the clean clothes Eli had left for him and shook James awake.

"What's happening?" James jolted, almost knocking his forehead into Sebastian's.

"Whoa there." Sebastian steadied him. "I'm free to go."

James beamed, his smile so bright it was almost blinding, and pulled Sebastian into his lap. "Wonderful."

"Yes, it is. I'm all better, so you can quit worrying so hard."

"I wasn't worrying hard, just a very reasonable amount."

"Okay, if you say so." Sebastian wiped a bit of drool from the corner of James's mouth. "Now, take me home, please."

James tangled a hand in Sebastian's curls and brought their lips together. "That's exactly what I plan to do, sweetheart. But let's make a little detour first."

After leaving the hospital—Eli and Parker had brought James's truck and some fresh clothes down for him—James drove Sebastian to the burrito place they'd meant to go to what felt like a lifetime ago.

Sitting in the passenger seat, Sebastian couldn't say he remembered the last time he'd been in the truck, driving from Storm House to Parker's. He didn't even remember leaving the Storm House property. The final events of that night had taken on a nightmarish quality in his mind and didn't seem entirely real, but Sebastian didn't mind it feeling like a fever dream. He would rather focus on what came next and how happy he was it was all over than the fight it took to get here.

He was free. Completely, and unlike when he'd first escaped Storm House, his feelings weren't complicated. Sebastian felt light and giddy. He was no longer scared of his future. He wasn't scared to be happy or trying to push away his feelings for James. He was all in for what life had in store for him.

The burrito place was packed when James pulled up so Sebastian opted to stay in the truck while James ordered for them. His social anxiety seemed to be here to stay, and while he was game for going into the restaurant next time, when he wasn't fresh out of the hospital, Sebastian wasn't angry about his reactions like he had been at first. He didn't mind if he did things differently now than he had before.

James returned with a brown paper bag and two sodas. "Think you can hold off eating a bit longer?"

Sebastian looked longingly at the bag. The food smelled amazing. "Potentially."

James started the truck. "I promise it will be worth it."

Sebastian picked up his drink. "Are we going somewhere special?"

"Yeah." He threw Sebastian a sweet smile. "Put on some music."

Sebastian connected his phone to the truck's Bluetooth. "You need to learn the lyrics to this album, just FYI."

James laughed. "Okay, but don't say I didn't warn you when you hear me sing. It's not going to be pretty."

Sebastian couldn't figure out where they were going at first. He hadn't been past Apple Valley in this direction since high school. By the end of the album, he figured they had to be getting close to the coast.

James pulled onto a dirt road. Sebastian rolled down his window and smelled the fresh salt air.

"We're going to the beach," Sebastian said in awe, like he'd never been there before. It had been so long this might as well have been his first time.

The ocean came into view and Sebastian drank in the sight. The sea breeze ruffled his curls, and he was tempted to stick his head out the window.

James pulled over in a turn-out and backed up so the rear of the truck faced the ocean. "It'd be better if I had some blankets." He jumped out and opened the tailgate.

Sebastian followed with the food and James's drink. He'd already finished his.

James arranged a drop cloth he must use at work sites in the truck bed and patted it invitingly. "Hop on up."

Sebastian did so. "This is perfect."

"Yeah, it is." James leaned in for a kiss before sitting next to Sebastian.

They reheated the food with a quick spell and ate, watching the waves and birds pecking around in the sand. The air was so fresh. Sebastian had no idea how much he'd missed the sea. He'd never been a huge beach person, even in San Diego, but being here at this moment felt so right. Nothing said freedom like looking out at the vast expanse of water.

Sebastian dug into his food. "This might be the best meal I've ever tasted."

"I have to agree. Though everything feels so good right now that I think I'd have said that even if I was eating dirt."

Sebastian swatted James's shoulder. "That is not the visual I wanted."

"Sorry." James swiped a bit of salsa from the corner of Sebastian's mouth. "Let's never talk about being underground or in the earth ever again."

"Deal." Sebastian took another bite of his chili relleno burrito, swinging his legs back and forth off the edge of the truck bed. "Unless we're talking about gardening. Then dirt and being in the earth will play a pretty important role."

James laughed. "I can't wait to talk about gardening."

"That's what I like to hear."

They finished their food and walked along the sand. It was cold but not too windy. Sebastian's hand was sore and he felt a bit off-balance when he looked at it all bandaged up, but it didn't wipe the smile from his face. The afternoon was perfect, and nothing could change that.

THEY RETURNED to Moonlight Falls that evening. While it had been lovely to get out and see the ocean, Sebastian was happy to be home.

That made for a first, and Sebastian could have laughed at himself, but it really did feel good to be in Moonlight Falls. There was a calming undercurrent to the area he swore he hadn't noticed before. Perhaps it was the magic that all the die-hard Moonlighters swore by, and Sebastian had never noticed it with all the strong negative emotions the town had always triggered in him. Or maybe it felt good because he was coming home with James to a place where he had friends and was beginning to belong.

He hadn't forgotten the angry mob, but now wasn't the time to dwell on those particular people.

"Is Eli home?" Sebastian asked as they got out of the truck.

"I think he's at Parker's." James led the way into the house. "Maybe we can go see everyone tomorrow?"

"Sounds good to me." Sebastian wasn't in the mood for anything with the group tonight. He needed to figure out how much James had told everyone and if they'd have questions for him. He wouldn't mind answering them, but he didn't want to get sucked too deep into memories of that night at Storm House.

"Hey." James brushed back Sebastian's bangs. "What's going on in there?" He tapped Sebastian's forehead.

"Just thinking about telling everyone all the gory details." He tried to make light, but it didn't seem like James bought it.

"I've told them everything they need to know. Gory details spared. They know you saved all our lives and that you were brave as fuck."

Sebastian repressed a smile. "You would tell them that."

"It's the truth." James's gaze turned thoughtful. "If you ever want to talk about what you went through or what we went through, all you have to do is let me know."

"Same goes for you." Sebastian flexed his bandaged hand. "It was a lot. Dealing with the curse and everything surrounding it is going to have lingering effects on all of us. I'm prepared to deal with it, look into some trauma therapy or whatever, but I'm not prepared to be stuck in the past. I don't want to dwell on it. I want to move on."

"I'm right there with you." James's hand found its way to the small of Sebastian's back. "On that note, how does an early night and a fresh start in the morning sound?"

"Like heaven."

They stripped, had a much-needed shower, and crawled into James's bed. Sebastian snuggled up to James, his head on James's firm chest.

"Thank you for standing by me," Sebastian whispered.

"Of course, sweetheart. I'll always be here for you."

"And I'll always be here for you, James." Sebastian smiled into James's skin, his familiar smell soothing. They had each other, and that was all that truly mattered.

SEBASTIAN

They'd fallen asleep so early that Sebastian woke at midnight feeling relatively well-rested, even if it took him a moment to figure out he was in James's bed. He couldn't remember any of the last week, and for a second, he wasn't sure if the darkness outside was natural or a sign the shades had reinvaded.

The throbbing in his hand cleared things up, triggering a flood of memories.

Sebastian got up and took something for the pain. What happened in the woods was harrowing, but he was able to focus on his success and the immense relief of having it all behind him. He was in a place he feared he'd never reach and wouldn't stop being overjoyed to have his life back.

As he climbed back into bed, James stirred.

"What time is it?" James mumbled.

"The middle of the night, babe. Go back to sleep."

James cracked an eye open. "You good?"

"A little sore, but I'm fine."

James wrapped his arms around Sebastian and buried his face in Sebastian's neck. "Want me to take your mind off it?"

Sebastian ran a hand down James's bare back. "How were you thinking?"

"I was having the most vivid dream," he murmured, kissing Sebastian's throat.

"Oh, were you?" Sebastian arched his neck, smiling wide. "Tell me more."

"You were balls deep inside me, fucking me on the beach." James pressed against Sebastian, and sure enough, he was hard.

Sebastian groaned. "I love your imagination."

"I love waking up naked with you, knowing we can make it all a reality. Well, maybe not the beach part. There was a distinct lack of inconveniently placed sand in the dream."

Sebastian snorted.

James lifted his head, finding Sebastian's gaze. "How about I blow you? That should make you feel good."

Sebastian rested his bandaged hand against James's cheek. "Fucking you would feel good too."

Heat darkened James's eyes. "I want you inside me so badly right now, but maybe we should wait."

"For what, marriage?"

James choked on a laugh. "No, for you to heal."

"It's my finger, not my dick. I think I can manage to fuck you without hurting it."

"I know, I just feel a bit rude asking you to do all the work. You only just got out of the hospital. I've been out for days."

Sebastian gave him an evil grin. "Oh, I'm happy for you to do all the work, babe."

James's eyes flashed. "Ah. I was stuck on the position from my dream, on all fours. I hadn't even thought of riding you."

Longing coursed through Sebastian. "Well, we're both thinking it now."

James groaned, reaching between Sebastian's legs and clasping his half-hard cock. "I want you so much. Having you inside me will be like screwing everything we had to do to get here."

"I love that," Sebastian gasped as James stroked him to full hardness.

"I love you." James captured Sebastian's mouth in a deep, languid kiss. He rolled Sebastian on his back and straddled him, continuing his drawn-out kisses.

Sebastian melted. He loved that James had been dreaming about him and had shared it rather than not saying anything. He couldn't wait to get James on all fours and make him scream in pleasure. Not at the beach, he had to agree, but maybe in the garden of his imaginary new house, the sun on their backs in a perfect reverse-recreation of one memorable afternoon they'd had at Storm House, trapped and waiting for the fuel cell to arrive with nothing to do but get each other off.

James had fucked Sebastian in his garden and made Sebastian see stars. Those days waiting in limbo before they escaped the property had been strangely wonderful, and Sebastian planned to take all the good from that time and bring it forward, leaving the rest behind.

Dreaming of the future felt like a gift, and Sebastian couldn't wait to make every idea bursting in his mind a reality, but tonight, he preferred slow and sensual to the wild images filling his head. Like the one of James on his knees in the grass next to blooming flowers, moaning as Sebastian pounded into him.

One day…

As James got up to find the lube, Sebastian propped himself against the headboard. He pulled James into his lap and held him close, just feeling him, breathing him in, and getting lost in all the little things.

Sebastian stroked James's stubble-rough cheek. "Can I watch you get yourself ready for me?"

James paused. "I want to see you, not be facing away."

"Me too. Do it like this." Sebastian cradled James's hips,

sliding one hand around to his ass and finding his hole. "Sit on my lap and open yourself up while I kiss you."

James smiled almost shyly. "I can do that."

James squirted lube on his fingers and reached behind himself. Sebastian moved his fingers out of the way and let James touch himself, opting to stroke James's cock instead. James let out a soft moan, his other hand braced around the back of Sebastian's neck. His fingers flexed on Sebastian's nape and his eyes fluttered closed.

Sebastian was enraptured. James touching himself was beautiful. He was so open and needy, his expressions shaping his face freely, letting Sebastian see exactly how he felt. Sebastian ached for him. The way James rocked into his hand, dick leaking on Sebastian's stomach, felt even more intimate than when Sebastian had been the one stretching James.

"Almost there," James panted, getting more lube. Sebastian got some on his own hand and reached back along with James. As James realized what Sebastian was up to, he whimpered. "Yes," he pleaded, leaning his forehead against Sebastian's.

Sebastian slipped a finger in beside James's two, his hand covering James's. They moaned in unison, and James leaned forward, sealing their lips in a kiss. Sebastian rested his bandaged hand on the back of James's neck, pain forgotten, as they fingered James's hole together.

James broke the kiss. "Now, Sebastian. Please."

Sebastian smiled, filled with pure joy, as he slicked himself up. James had a desperate, almost hungry look as he lined himself up, holding Sebastian in place as he sank down, letting out a soft whimper.

It was Sebastian's favorite sound. This one, in particular, was different from the noises James made when he topped Sebastian. It was something unique that only the two of them together in this specific way could create.

"I love you, James," Sebastian crooned, his voice thick with pleasure.

"I love you," James echoed before dropping his head back and swiveling his hips.

Sebastian gasped in pleasure. "You feel so perfect, James."

James let out another of those little whimpers, and Sebastian got lost in the rhythm of James's hips.

They'd had no small amount of sex up to this point, but nothing like this. In many ways, it was a miracle they were here, together, expressing their deepest feelings. It felt like the true beginning of something, with all their worst obstacles stripped away. The rest of their lives had started, and Sebastian couldn't wait.

THE NEXT MORNING, Sebastian and James walked into town. The air was brisk and the sky was steadily clouding over. All Sebastian could think was it felt great to be out in the fresh air.

"I've always liked being outside, but I think staying in the hospital has given me a new appreciation for it," Sebastian said as they crunched leaves under their feet, passing the school.

Everything was back to normal in Moonlight Falls. The school had reopened after its brief closure, and everyone who had evacuated seemed to have returned without delay. People here really were unfazed by unusual occurrences and more tolerant than most to a bit of horror. Sebastian didn't doubt that anywhere else, people would have been reluctant to return after the darkness, vein-induced earthquakes, vicious shade attacks, and possessions. But not here. Moonlight Falls was home.

They walked into the town circle, hand in hand. Something immediately caught Sebastian's eye near the stone. It looked like signs and flowers had been placed in the grass.

He turned to James. "It's not election season, is it?"

"No." James's brow furrowed as they approached the grass.

Sebastian read the phrase painted on the largest sign: *Thank you, Sebastian Storm, for saving Moonlight Falls*. It was covered in puff-paint hearts that looked like they'd been done by someone's child.

Sebastian stopped, dead still. *"What?"* He turned to James. "Did you know about this?"

James beamed, his eyes glassy. "No. I had no idea. I knew Eleanor addressed the town. Parker said the town hall meeting was so packed there were people out in the street. She told everyone that you saved Moonlight Falls from exploding by fixing the broken veins and fighting off the invading shades. I don't know who put all this here, but it looks like lots of people are grateful for what you did."

One sign proclaimed Sebastian a hero. He had no idea what to think of it. Another sign said *Moonlight Falls commends the Storm family for keeping us safe*.

"They're pretty forgiving of the fact that the Storms started the problem with the veins," Sebastian muttered, still in shock.

"I think it's nice they're acknowledging the sacrifice you all made for the town." James wrapped an arm around Sebastian's waist. "The whole mess with the curse is complicated, with no easy rights or wrongs. There's no doubt your family did more than anyone should have had to for this town, even if they accidentally started it all."

"True." Sebastian stared at a bunch of roses laying in the grass. "I'm glad people know the truth about Stephen and the family. We do deserve a bit of acknowledgment."

"You're an important part of Moonlight Falls, sweetheart. You and your family helped shape this place and kept it safe."

"Even if we were the ones to let the shades in," Sebastian replied dryly.

James shrugged. "The gateway wasn't a problem for eighty years, and it helped us establish a solid bit of tourism."

Sebastian smiled at James's optimistic take on the situation. "Wonder what we'll do about that tourism now that shades won't be popping through from Beyond all the time."

James considered. "I'm sure everyone will adjust. It'll be strange to not have shades around Moonlight Falls, but after the last weeks, I won't be complaining."

"Sebastian!" a voice called from behind them, stealing their attention.

Sebastian spun to see his mom exiting the diner. "She's still here?" He couldn't believe it.

"Yeah, I wasn't expecting to see her again," James agreed.

"Sebastian." Samantha stopped a few feet from them, looking between him and James as if she was unsure how to approach. "I'm glad you're all right."

"You are?" Sebastian asked without thinking.

She flinched. "Yes. I can't believe any of us survived that." Her eyes strayed to the signs, then back to Sebastian, conflicted emotion lining her face. "I'm sorry for accusing you of trapping me. And I'm sorry for putting all this on you, for transferring the curse, and for how I let that dictate the way I treated you all these years. I'm sorry for all of it and for not trying to make it right."

Sebastian let himself absorb her words. He sighed. "I appreciate you saying that." And he did. Even if it couldn't undo the past or change anything, her apology gave Sebastian a small sense of relief.

Samantha fidgeted. "I didn't want to leave before saying something."

Sebastian gave her a tired smile. "It was a nice surprise."

She returned his smile. It looked slightly pained. "I'm glad you get to live the rest of your life free from this. I hope you'll be happy."

"Thanks. I think I will be." Sebastian took James's hand. The moment had a strong undercurrent of awkwardness. He valued his mom's apology but wasn't going to tell her it was all right or act like it was enough to forgive everything she'd done and go on as if it had never happened.

"I owe you an apology too, James." Samantha looked at her shoes. "I'm sorry for my part in your parents' deaths."

James gave a curt nod as if his feelings mirrored Sebastian's.

"If there's anything you want me to do… I know I can't make up for it, but…" Her words seemed to fail.

James's attention found Sebastian. He seemed unsure how to react. Sebastian squeezed James's hand, and James turned back to Samantha, clearing his throat. "The secret-binding is completely gone. Nothing is stopping the truth from coming out."

Samantha's eyes widened. "You want me to admit we caused the accident publicly?"

"I don't know." James swiped a hand over his face. "Just don't lie about it when it comes out."

"People are going to find out the whole story," Sebastian reminded his mom. "The transfer of the curse from Kira to me, our connection to Nelson Power, all of it. I'm not interested in hiding family history when what happened with the Storms affected everyone."

Samantha seemed to gather herself. "I won't ask you to. But I'm not planning to stay and endure the town's hatred."

"No, I wouldn't have thought so." Sebastian knew his mother wouldn't completely change. There was no magic to heal their relationship, and after everything, he didn't need there to be. "Guess this is goodbye then."

Samantha nodded, eyes lingering on Sebastian's bandage for a second. "Goodbye, Sebastian."

He watched her walk to the bed and breakfast and disappear inside.

James leaned in close. "You okay?"

"It's the best I could have hoped for. I wasn't exactly

holding out for us to reconnect and have the mother-son bond I once longed for. I'd much rather make my own family."

"You've already got one."

Sebastian turned to face James and found a delicate smile on his face.

"I think a few of them are at the diner now if you feel like stopping in?"

Warmth bloomed in Sebastian's chest. "In that case, a late breakfast sounds perfect."

The diner was bound to be quiet at eleven a.m. on a Tuesday, and he had his headphones around his neck in case the noise started to put him on edge. "Let's go bother Eli and Parker. I have to thank them for getting us to the hospital. It completely slipped my mind before."

They crossed the street and Sebastian opened the diner door, ringing the bell. Eli leaped from behind the counter and rushed to them.

"Sebastian!" Eli threw his arms around him, and Sebastian returned the hug without hesitation. "I'm so glad you're out of the hospital."

"Feels good to be free. Thanks for getting us there."

"Of course." Eli gave him one more squeeze before moving on to James. "Good to see you back in town too."

James ruffled Eli's hair. "Nothing can keep me away long."

Parker exited the kitchen and didn't delay giving Sebastian his own near-crushing hug. "Good to see you on your feet."

Sebastian's face was hot from all the attention, but he didn't mind. The only other person in the place seemed to be Princeton, sitting alone at the opposite end of the room.

"My feet weren't exactly the problem," Sebastian joked.

Parker released him, a hand lingering on his shoulder. "How's your finger?"

"Pretty much completely gone." Sebastian lifted his bandaged hand. "The doctors expect it to heal fine now that they fixed the mess I made of it."

Parker squeezed Sebastian's shoulder, looking him in the eye with that intimidating expression of his. "Thank you."

"For?" Sebastian's gaze flitted instinctually to James, then back to Parker.

"For making a sacrifice for us and for the town."

"Oh." Sebastian squirmed, and Parker withdrew his hand. "You don't have to thank me."

"For cutting off your finger to save us, I think we do," Eli argued.

To Sebastian, it didn't feel like a huge deal, not compared to having to give up his life, but maybe James hadn't told the others about that part of the night. They didn't know how far he'd been willing to go.

"Everyone in town is grateful," Parker went on, gesturing to the display around the stone. "Even if Eleanor didn't broadcast specifically what sacrifice you had to make. She kept the details out of it, making sure your privacy was respected, but everyone knows you did something brave for them."

Sebastian stared at the hand-painted signs, glad his missing finger wasn't the talk of the town. "They aren't going to forget it any time soon, are they?"

James studied him. "Does the attention make you uncomfortable?"

"A bit," Sebastian admitted. "But not in a bad way. It's nice to be appreciated. It makes me feel like I've been accepted."

"You have been," Parker said resolutely. "I've already had people ask when I'm putting your photo up in the diner."

Sebastian's mouth fell open. "*My photo?*"

Parker and Eli grinned, the big man hooking his thumbs in the pockets of his apron. "A key piece of town history like you vanquishing horrible shade-beings and stopping the veins from blasting the place off the map has to be celebrated."

Sebastian was overwhelmed with pleasurable embarrassment. He wasn't a fan of too much attention—he found it stressful—but when it came with the sense of belonging and accomplishment he had right now, he didn't mind so much.

James studied him, an understanding expression on his face like he knew exactly what Sebastian was feeling. "We could take a picture right now, out by the stone."

"You have to be in it with me." Sebastian pulled James against him.

"Anything you want, sweetheart," James agreed before turning a calculated look on Parker. "Speaking of pictures, we could replace my old photo with this new one. I can't be up there twice."

"No, you can't take it down. I like it," Sebastian whined, tightening his grip on James. "I won't let mine be put up if you get rid of yours."

Parker nodded approvingly. "Good call."

James laughed. "Fine. If everyone likes the damn photo so much, I'll stop complaining."

"Really?" Eli gave him a weird look. "You've complained for ten years. You're really going to give in *now*?"

James gazed adoringly at Sebastian. "Yes. How could I complain about something that makes this man smile?"

Sebastian kissed him. A quick, hard peck. "Careful." He felt his smile turn devious. "You know I'm going take advantage of that."

"I can't wait," James whispered.

Sebastian loved him so much he didn't know if he'd ever stop being amazed by it.

They went outside, and Eli took a picture of Sebastian and James in front of the stone and the signs. He even snapped a few extra as James dipped Sebastian into a kiss, one of Sebastian's legs flinging into the air in surprise.

Eventually, they returned to the diner to eat.

"What happened with you all that night?" Sebastian asked Eli after Parker disappeared into the kitchen.

"We pretty much hunkered down." A frown pulled at Eli's lips. "Hazel and Eleanor were with us at Parker's. I tried to call you guys, but it must have been after you went to Storm House. When the tremors stopped, we were so relieved, but you still didn't turn up or answer your phones. I wanted to go look for you both, but so many shades were flying around town that we couldn't leave the house. We were lucky they didn't attack any of the buildings."

"I'm glad you were safe." Sebastian was immensely relieved. He'd have hated for everyone to have been stuck fighting shades while he and James figured out how to fix the veins. Digging up those graves took a hell of a long time. Sebastian was thankful it was all a blur in his mind now.

Eventually, Eli left them to eat and went back to his work.

A dull ache started behind Sebastian's eyes. He must have made a face because James caught on.

"Headache?"

Sebastian nodded. "It's not bad, but after this, I might be done with being in public for the day."

The doctors had told Sebastian his headaches might be a permanent side effect of using the veins' power. They couldn't be totally sure since no one had harnessed power like that before, and they didn't know exactly what it might do to someone's body.

Sebastian hadn't had any pain as severe as he'd had that night or even the days in between first using the veins and when it was all over. He was taking that as a good sign, hoping that now that the veins were repaired and he wasn't a piece of them, the headaches wouldn't be as bad.

The bell above the door sounded, and Hazel and Eleanor walked in.

Sebastian smiled. It seemed he could take a bit more socializing after all.

The two women joined him and James in their booth and asked how he was.

"I cannot thank you enough," Eleanor said once the catching-up was out of the way. "This town owes you."

"Don't worry about it. Really," Sebastian insisted. "No one owes me. It's not a debt that needs to be repaid."

Eleanor smiled. "You'll have to take our eternal gratitude anyway."

"I suppose I can deal with that," Sebastian relented, that pleasurable embarrassment returning, making his cheeks hot.

"I hope it goes some way to making up for William's behavior," Eleanor continued, her familiar, serious demeanor making an appearance.

Sebastian scrunched his nose. "What happened with him?"

Eleanor and Hazel exchanged a glance. "He's been arrested for inciting a riot and assault, along with breaking and entering. The people who went along with him have been arrested too."

Sebastian was relieved to hear it. "I'm glad no one's getting away with it."

"No, of course not. It was awful." Eleanor gave him an understanding look.

"What about the possession?" James asked.

Hazel shook her head. "William tried to say the shade made him do all of it and he wasn't in his right mind, but no one's taking his word for it. He can use possession as a defense in court if he wants, but it was pretty obvious when the shade inside him was acting. Parker said his eyes went black and he had the pointy teeth and everything."

"Yeah, I had the impression he organized the angry mob himself," Sebastian agreed. "I wonder how long he was possessed."

James grabbed Sebastian's arm. "Remember the night we saw

William leaving town hall and a shade flew up to him but didn't bother him?" Sebastian nodded. "What if he was possessed then, and that's why the shade didn't attack."

"Could be. But then he might be able to pin everything from the B&E to the riot on being possessed."

"I don't think so," Eleanor countered. "William had already shown he was willing to turn people against you at the town hall meeting, and regardless of when exactly he became possessed, Hazel is right. It was obvious when the shade was controlling him."

"You don't have to worry about him, Sebastian." Hazel gave him a comforting pat on the arm. "I doubt he'll ever be back in Moonlight Falls, even if he manages to avoid prison."

"No one here will be happy to see him again," Eleanor agreed. "I doubt he'd want to face the scorn of the rest of the people in town. They won't want anyone bothering you."

Sebastian repressed a smile. Moonlight Falls had well and truly chosen him. He was home.

27

JAMES

"Where are we going?" Sebastian asked James from the passenger seat of his truck the next day.

James had the entire week off work. He owed Hazel a serious vacation after all this. He just had to find a way to convince her to actually take one. Maybe he could get Eleanor to persuade her.

James threw Sebastian a mischievous look. "Can it be a surprise?"

"Hm. I guess. As long as no one is going to jump out at me screaming '*Surprise!*'"

"It's not that kind, I promise," he assured Sebastian.

"Okay." Sebastian still sounded suspicious, but he settled back in his seat and let James drive him through the east side of town. "I should probably get my expired driver's license renewed at some point, or you'll be stuck driving me everywhere, surprise or not."

"You know I don't mind, but we can sort it out when we're in Apple Valley for your follow-up appointment." James turned down Pine Street.

"Hey, this is where Eli sent his skateboard through the darkness."

"It is." James eyed Sebastian as he pulled over.

Sebastian turned away from the window. "This is that plot of land for sale."

James blushed, even if he wasn't sure why. "Yeah, a whole acre and a half. I called the realtor this morning and she said the people next door are planning on listing their house in the spring but are happy for us to come check it out today."

"Next door?" Sebastian spun back to the window. "Oh, it's a cute house. Look at the front porch. It has a swing."

James smiled at the excitement in Sebastian's voice. "I figured the house plus the extra land would give you your hobby farm."

Sebastian nodded enthusiastically. "Miss Moo will love it, and it's so close to town. I can even see the neighbors."

"I'm glad you like it already."

Sebastian unbuckled his seatbelt. "It might actually be perfect. The forest is just over there, but not too close. I can plant my fruit trees and have a huge garden, though we'll need that hedged in for privacy."

"We will?"

Sebastian grinned slyly. "I thought we could have a repeat of our last garden romp."

Heat settled low in James's belly as he remembered that particular idle day in the sun at Storm House. "I like where your head is at. As long as we're switching positions. I haven't been able to get that dream out of my head."

Sebastian patted James's cheek. "Don't worry about that, babe." He glanced out the window again. "We're definitely far enough from the neighbors. They won't hear you scream my name."

"Oh my god, it's a good thing the realtor isn't here yet." James willed his blush to go away.

Sebastian cackled with glee.

Once the realtor arrived, she walked them through the four-bedroom house. Sebastian bounced along, bursting with energy. He liked the layout of the house and the size and already had all kinds of ideas for renovations. He'd redo the kitchen, add a sunroom out back. He even declared a need for more outdoor storage and James caught him looking up prefabricated sheds and barns on his phone.

"I can see you're interested," the realtor hedged. "The owners said they were open to shifting their moving plans forward if you wanted to buy before the spring."

"Excellent. Do you have a business card?" Sebastian asked as he inspected the largest bedroom's en suite.

She handed one over and went outside to give them a bit of space.

"This shower really isn't big enough," Sebastian mused. "I'll need to expand to fit a tub in here anyway, so I might as well redo the shower while I'm at it."

James took in the standard, well-looked-after bathroom. "I feel like you're recreating your Storm House bathroom."

Sebastian shrugged. "What can I say? I've gotten used to the clawfoot tub, and you need to be able to fit in the shower with me."

"All good points." James followed Sebastian into the bedroom, down the hall, and through to the open-plan living and dining area. "Your piano would fit well in here."

"That's a great idea." Sebastian walked across the dining space. "I don't need a big table. There's room in the kitchen for a small one and outside for a large picnic table." His brow wrinkled.

"What is it?"

Sebastian looked down at his bandage. "I wasn't thinking about playing piano when I cut my finger off. I'm going to have to relearn how to play. Damn, I wish I'd thought to use one of my toes."

"I'm sorry, sweetheart."

Sebastian looked up, his expression surprisingly light. "Don't be. I'll still be able to play. It's just going to take practice."

James smiled. "I love watching you at the piano."

"Yeah, but you'd watch me do anything."

James rolled his eyes. "I would, but I especially like hearing you play. You're very talented."

Sebastian's cheeks tinged pink, and he was almost bashful during the rest of their time in the house.

Back in the truck, Sebastian turned to James. "Is it too impulsive to buy the first house I look at?"

"I don't know if it's impulsive. You've thought about what you want. If you're sure living in Moonlight Falls is for you, and you like this house and land as much as you seemed to, I don't see why you shouldn't go for it. You've waited long enough."

"I have waited long enough, haven't I? I think I'm going to do it. I know I want to be in Moonlight Falls. There's no question about that, and this house is pretty much perfect."

James wondered what Sebastian would do with Storm House. He figured the question could wait for another day. It was nice focusing forward. There was no rush to do anything with the old property.

James's phone buzzed and he checked the incoming text. "Eli wants us to meet him in town."

"Sounds good." Sebastian buckled his seatbelt, and James pulled onto the road. "I want to go talk to Mila anyway. I'm going to see if she needs a volunteer for the library."

"I'm sure she does. They've been talking about bringing back the after-school programs, though I don't know if they've been able to get anyone to run them."

"Oh yay. I loved the kid stuff they used to do. I feel like I'd be good at dramatic readings of picture books."

"I feel like you would be too." James paused, grinning as he pictured it. "Is that what you want to do?"

"I think so, at least for now. I don't exactly need a paycheck. Nelson Power is going to keep me and any future Storms fed and clothed for a while."

James pulled into the parking lot behind the diner. He liked the idea of future Storms. He let himself imagine having a family with Sebastian, and the possibility tugged on his heart. Sebastian would be a wonderful father.

They found Eli by the stone, a familiar portable magical energy flow meter in his hand.

"Hey, guys." Eli waved them closer. They maneuvered around the signs and flowers on the grass to reach him.

"You don't let anything keep you from studying, do you?" James teased.

"No." Eli gave him a look like, *why would I?* "I had the longest video call with my supervisor last week, explaining the veins and everything I couldn't tell him before. He thinks I should change my enrollment and transfer to a PhD. I have more than enough for a research proposal at that level now."

"Wow, that's great." James clapped him on the shoulder.

Eli brimmed with excitement, smiling widely. "I'm going to do a complete study of the vein intersection and see if I can publish an article on the imbalance. There's so much to do. I'm testing out a new theory now."

Sebastian eyed the magical flow meter. "Is that why you wanted to see us?"

"Yeah." Eli gestured to the stone. "I was trying to see what the deal was with this."

James frowned at the large rock, unable to quell his suspicion. He'd never see it the same way after the shades used it in their attacks on Moonlight Falls. "Does the stone have magic?"

"No, it doesn't have any of its own, but I think it can conduct magic."

"Like how some things conduct electricity?" James asked.

"Yeah, I guess." Eli shrugged. "The vein running below the stone must make contact with it. I'd love to dig and see how deep the stone goes, but it seems like it's conducting magical energy from the vein, bringing it to the surface. I've been able to detect trace amounts in the air around the stone, which is something you wouldn't normally see. Vein energy is always contained within the earth."

"Huh." James frowned more severely at the rock, Sebastian doing the same.

"But that's not my theory."

James returned his focus to Eli. "What's your theory?"

"You know how everyone says they can feel the magic of Moonlight Falls?" Eli waited for James and Sebastian to nod. "Well, maybe they can. If the stone brings the veins' magic to the surface, people could very well be feeling it. *And* I'd bet money that it being magic from a fixed vein intersection with a rare straight formation makes it special. That's why Moonlight Falls feels like nowhere else."

"So the stone is like a beacon?" Sebastian asked. "That actually makes a lot of sense. People aren't the only ones drawn here. One of the shades said they'd been called. What if the stone bringing the unique magic to the surface attracted shades as well as people. They may have been able to sense it through the gateway."

"That's a great point." Eli pulled a notebook out of a backpack, discarded the bag on the ground, and began writing. "I can't wait to record all the unique properties of this vein intersection. Even with the imbalance fixed, it's an extraordinarily rare magical formation."

James caught Sebastian's eye, surprised to find Sebastian frowning. "What's up?"

"I was just thinking about my connection to the veins." Sebastian rubbed his head absently. "It'll be totally gone, right? I mean,

I know it felt like it was ripped away that night, but I don't trust anything I was feeling. There was too much pain and confusion."

James had assumed the connection was gone, though he supposed they didn't know for sure. "Do you want to check?"

"Kind of." Sebastian studied the stone. "I was still able to use the veins after making my sacrifice, but now that the veins are restored, that connection should be severed."

"I'd say you're right," Eli cut in. "The energy at the intersection looks normal now. I've been monitoring it. The veins are behaving how I'd expect now that the missing pieces have been returned. You'll no longer be part of the unit."

Sebastian closed his eyes. He concentrated for a long few minutes before he opened his eyes and smiled. "Yeah, it's gone," he said in relief. "Thank fuck for that. Now I can just be drawn to the magic here like everyone else and leave my link to Moonlight Falls there."

"As it should be." Eli patted Sebastian on the shoulder.

James eyed the rock beside them once more. "Hearing you talk about the stone makes me feel like a moth flying into a flame."

Sebastian laughed. "I'm going to think of that every time someone talks about being drawn to the magic here. Moonlight Falls, calling us home like moths to a flame. Aren't we all clever?"

James snorted, shoving Sebastian playfully in the shoulder. "So clever."

"Or you could think of it as fate. I mean, it is *magic*. Maybe we were all meant to be here." Eli shrugged, his cheeks going red. It was the closest James had ever heard Eli come to admitting he believed in the mystical side of the citizens' connection to Moonlight Falls.

"I like that." James slung one arm around Eli and the other around Sebastian. "We were all meant to be here, together."

"Agreed," said Sebastian, and Eli seemed pleased.

James gave them each a squeeze before releasing them, turning to Sebastian. "Should we go find Mila?"

"Actually, I want to talk to the museum curator first."

"Princeton?" Eli tucked his notebook away. "He should be back at the post office. He stopped by to talk to me earlier about getting all my research displayed. I said he might need more space, at least when I'm finished."

"You're interested in sharing your research?" Sebastian asked.

"Yeah. He asked me before, and I was inclined to blow him off, but I feel like people here will really like it. And if everything I learn is as unique as I think, it'll be of interest to a lot of people outside Moonlight Falls too."

Sebastian seemed excited by the idea. "I agree, and I might have some more questions for you about displays later, but we'll leave you to it for now."

"Okay." Eli nodded happily before turning back to his notebook.

James followed Sebastian toward the post office. "What do you want with Princeton?"

"I want to see if he'd like a new museum. A couple rooms attached to the post office isn't much."

James stopped in his tracks. "You mean Storm House?"

Sebastian shrugged, a hint of shyness in the motion. "Yeah. It'd be good to do something with the house. Have people out there again. And if Princeton wants to do the town history, what better place to display it than the property where the vein intersection lies? He can put the details of the Storm curse on display, let people see the house, and fill the many rooms with interesting stuff like natural history or the story of the town's founding or whatever. Not to mention Eli's research."

"That's a wonderful idea." James glowed with pride for Sebastian. It was a perfect and rather healing end to Storm House. "Princeton is going to be beside himself."

"This means you'll have to finish rewiring Storm House, you

know," Sebastian added in a conspiratorial tone. "Now that the power-draining issue has been solved, I can't expect a museum to function without electricity."

"Way to bring it back around, Sebastian." James looped an arm around his neck and pulled him in for a kiss on the cheek. "But I'm dragging Hazel out there with me this time, just to be safe."

"That's probably for the best. I hope she and Princeton like green."

28

SEBASTIAN

TWO MONTHS LATER.

MISS MOO LET out a snort of satisfaction and bent down to munch the grass. Sebastian patted her shoulder. She'd settled in nicely to her new home at 110 Pine Street.

"James will be here soon," Sebastian told the cow. "I'll make sure he says hello."

Miss Moo didn't acknowledge this, but then, she'd always liked Sebastian over James. It made sense after the years they'd had together.

Sebastian moved on to feeding the chickens. He'd painted their hutch red to match the brand-new barn at the far end of his property. Sebastian was going to leave green for the trees from here on out.

He collected the day's eggs and wandered back to the house. He loved it more than he should, given he'd only just moved in. He had plenty of renovations planned to make it his, but that was just the thing: this house was *his*. He was here because he'd chosen to be and could leave whenever. He just didn't think he'd want to.

Sebastian entered the kitchen and placed the eggs on the counter before setting the coffee brewing. The window above the counter had a perfect view of his vegetable garden, or what would eventually be his vegetable garden. At the moment, it was nothing but dirt and a pile of wood for planter beds.

He had an outdoor picnic area beside it and plans for a wood-fire pizza oven. Sebastian was going to ask Parker if he minded alternating Sunday dinners with him so the group could hang out here and Sebastian could cook for them all. He expected Parker to like the idea. He'd never failed to make Sebastian feel like part of the group.

Across the house, the front door opened, and James called, "Hi, Sebastian. I'm here."

"In the kitchen," he called back.

James appeared in a scruffy old hoodie and worn jeans, holding a brightly wrapped box in his arms.

Sebastian's attention snagged on the red bow. "What's that?"

"A housewarming gift." James offered up the box.

Sebastian grinned, taking it. "You didn't have to do that."

"I know." James gave one of his thoughtful frowns. "I wanted to. You moving into your dream home is an important occasion."

Sebastian set the box on the counter and wrapped his arms around James. "I love you."

James ran a hand through Sebastian's hair. "I love you too, sweetheart. I love seeing you this happy."

"These last couple of months have just been so nice. *So quiet.*"

James let out a deep sigh, pulling Sebastian closer. "I know. It's been even better than I imagined."

Moonlight Falls hadn't had any trouble since the night Sebastian restored the veins. Sebastian didn't know how many shades he'd sucked back into the gateway that night. He hadn't thought he'd recaptured the hundreds he'd seen streaming into the clearing, but if any of those beasts were still in this world, they seemed to have moved on from Moonlight Falls.

The gateway was closed, and while the humanoid shade Sebastian had fought could try to re-enter this world somewhere else, no one expected it to return to Moonlight Falls.

Eli theorized that the gateway at the intersection made it easier for the more intelligent beasts, like the ones that caused all the trouble, to pass between worlds than the usual shifting vein gateways. Therefore, it wasn't likely the humanoid shade could get back into the human world. It made sense since beasts like that were so rarely seen.

Sebastian also didn't think shades would enter through a shifting vein far away and bother traveling to Moonlight Falls just to try and take over again. He suspected the combination of the gateway and the unique magic of the vein intersection had made the town a target. If Beyond tried to stake its claim on this world again, they'd have to find some other hole to send their hordes through.

"Are you going to open your gift?" James asked, reminding Sebastian he had better things to think about.

Sebastian wiggled out of their embrace. "I suppose I should. Is it something sexy?"

A brief flash of uncertainty crossed James's face. "It's a house-warming gift. It's not supposed to be sexy."

Sebastian loved teasing James but didn't want him to think the gift was a disappointment. "You're totally right." He sent a reassuring smile James's way. "We can get each other sexy presents another time."

James seemed happily relieved. "I'll look forward to that."

Sebastian ripped the bow off and unwrapped the present. He opened the box to find a layer of tissue paper. He quirked a brow. "Is it clothes?"

James gave him a look of mock confusion. "If only there was a way for you to find out."

Sebastian swatted his arm and tore through the tissue paper. Beneath lay a purple robe. "Oh my gosh!" Sebastian lifted the garment out of the box. "How did you get this?" It wasn't the same robe he'd had stolen by the shade. It was an identical brand-new one.

James radiated smugness. "Now that's a secret I can't reveal."

Sebastian rubbed the silk fabric against his cheek. "You called my lawyer, didn't you?"

"Okay, maybe. But he wouldn't tell me where you got the original robe from. Apparently, all your shopping is confidential."

Sebastian laughed. "Poor guy is probably disappointed I'm not paying him to do every little thing for me now." He set the robe aside. "This is the best present. Thank you."

"I'm glad you like it. Happy housewarming." James leaned in and brushed his lips against Sebastian's. "We should probably get going."

"You're right. I'll get the travel mugs."

They fixed their coffees and left the house. Sebastian waved to Miss Moo before climbing into James's truck. He was happy to note James waved to the cow too.

"I'll have my license back soon, so you won't have to keep coming out here," Sebastian said as they pulled out of his driveway.

"I don't mind."

No, Sebastian supposed he didn't. James seemed to whole-heartedly love all the time he and Sebastian spent together. Maybe even more now than he had months ago, which Sebastian hadn't thought possible.

They drove through town and headed north. When James pulled up to the Storm House gate, the place was already buzzing with activity. The iron bars were propped open, the lock and chain having been discarded.

James drove onto the property and parked next to Hazel's new van. A group of workers were busy refinishing the outside of the house. A radio played on the porch, just loud enough to be heard over a whirring sander.

James and Hazel had been busy with the wiring while Sebastian helped Princeton organize the contents of the house. Some of the items they'd come across the museum curator wanted to keep and put on display. Sebastian was fine with that and let Princeton take the lead on deciding what to do with all the junk. They would have a large estate sale once they'd gone through it all, the proceeds going to the new museum. Anything that couldn't be sold or donated was being thrown out.

"It feels good bringing new life into this place," Sebastian said as he and James exited the truck.

"I bet." James opened the back and grabbed a box of tools.

A car rolled up the driveway behind them and came to a stop. Eleanor climbed out. "Sebastian, James, good to see you both."

James gave her a nod. "Wasn't expecting to find you here."

"I'm looking for Princeton." She took a moment to study Sebastian. "Though I'm glad I ran into you."

"Me?" Sebastian had spent the least amount of time with Eleanor out of everyone in their group. He wasn't sure what she'd need him for.

"Yes. I've been thinking. I know you're busy with the museum and the library at the moment, but once this place is finished, I figured you might have some time on your hands." She gestured to the house.

Sebastian shrugged. "It's going to be a while before that happens. Princeton and I haven't even gotten to the upstairs." Sebastian was donating the Storm House library contents to the museum, though they'd have to fish out all the X-rated material first.

"I don't doubt that." Eleanor smiled. "I just wanted to say, in case you were ever interested, the city council would love to have you."

Butterflies danced in Sebastian's stomach. "Really?"

"Of course. I don't know whether you're inclined to that sort of work, but I'd say the town would be happy to have you looking out for them. We'll have to elect someone soon to replace William, but his term was up next year anyway, so there'll be another vote then. Just some food for thought. I completely understand if you prefer working at the library."

"I'll think about it," Sebastian promised, possibilities blooming in the back of his mind.

"Great. Now, I better find Princeton." Eleanor walked up the porch steps and entered the house.

Eleanor's suggestion filled Sebastian with exhilaration. He'd love to be a part of Moonlight Falls, not just as a resident but as someone working for the town, putting his time and effort into this place.

"What do you think of that?" Sebastian asked James.

"I think you look excited."

Sebastian's cheeks heated. "I kinda like the idea."

"Me too." James squeezed his hand before lacing their fingers together, James's pinky and ring finger cradling the remaining knuckle of Sebastian's amputated finger. "You should go for it."

Sebastian buzzed as he considered it. "I might wait for the election next year. See how everything else goes first. But I'd love being a real part of this town."

James gazed at him with deep affection. "You already are, sweetheart."

29

JAMES

James stepped out of the shower and grabbed a towel. He was surprised Sebastian hadn't followed him into the bathroom once he'd turned the water on. Sebastian loved showering with him, and ever since they'd moved in together, Sebastian joined him in the steam-filled, spaciously built tile shower every weekend morning.

It was the most luxurious shower James had ever been in. Sebastian really knew how to spoil him. James loved the home Sebastian had created and all the little comforts Sebastian had indulged in.

There had been no question James would move into Sebastian's home when they were ready. He'd loved his grandmother's house, but it had always been her house, not his. Eli felt the same and had moved into Parker's place when they had made that step last year.

James and Eli had sold their grandmother's house when James

239

moved out, and driving by, seeing the new family living there, always made James smile.

He and Eli were both the happiest they'd ever been in Moonlight Falls. Gray Electrical was doing well, though James missed Hazel now that she was on an extended honeymoon in Europe with Eleanor. Eli was busy as ever with his research on the veins and traveling the country giving guest lectures on his findings. People came from all over to see his displays in the Storm House Museum and the veins themselves.

Then there was Sebastian. He might have been the most settled in and content of them all. He volunteered at the library every weekend and had won in a landslide for the city council position last year. James could see him being mayor one day and had a feeling Sebastian could picture it too.

James wiggled his toes on the heated tiles of his and Sebastian's bathroom. He loved this house more than he ever thought possible for a building, but of course, Sebastian had molded it into what it was, so James shouldn't have been surprised he adored it.

Exiting the bathroom, James expected to find Sebastian lazing in bed, maybe even asleep, explaining why he hadn't joined James in the shower. He was nowhere to be seen.

Something was up, but James had no idea what. There had been a few times recently when Sebastian had seemed distracted. He'd insisted it was nothing for James to worry about. James trusted him, and he wasn't worried, but he was suspicious.

Sebastian was planning something.

He'd thrown James a surprise thirtieth birthday party, and James had been completely shocked, though looking back, he was able to pick out the signs Sebastian had been scheming. This could be something similar, but with James's birthday passed, he wasn't sure what it could be about.

James dressed and wandered into the kitchen. It was Saturday morning, and he had no plans for the day.

Sebastian wasn't in the kitchen either. James frowned.

He turned back the way he'd come and checked the music nook by the piano. No Sebastian there or in the living room. He wasn't in the study, the game room, or the guest bedroom. He had to be outside, so James returned to the kitchen to wait for him to come back with the day's eggs.

James started making coffee, only to be thwarted when the pot wasn't in the percolator, the sink, or anywhere to be seen. *What the hell?* He looked outside, but Sebastian wasn't in the picnic area. He had to have taken the coffee pot, but if he'd put together breakfast outside, he should have been at their large outdoor table. It was a warm enough day for it.

James slipped on his shoes and went outside. He'd find his boyfriend somewhere. He wandered through the fruit trees into the back garden, which was full of flowers, lined with well-tended hedges, and looking absolutely beautiful this spring.

It was their private place, a little haven you could sit in and forget the rest of the world existed. Sebastian loved to get away from everything. He liked his quiet as long as he knew he could get up and go into town at any moment.

There Sebastian was, sitting on a picnic blanket by the daffodils. It was his favorite spot back here. James's, too, if he were honest. They'd had more than a few intimate moments among the flowers.

"Found you," James called as he approached.

"I was beginning to wonder." Sebastian looked up, the soft morning light catching the gold highlights in his ginger hair. "You took your time."

"Sorry." James smiled as he sat on the blanket. "I didn't know we had breakfast plans."

Sebastian blushed. He had the coffee pot on a wooden tray with two mugs next to a picnic basket. He seemed almost nervous. "I just thought it would be nice."

"It is," James insisted. "You're always so sweet, treating me to moments like this." James had plans to create the sweetest moment for Sebastian too—big plans—but he had to wait another two weeks for them to fall into place.

Sebastian shot James a look from under his lashes. "I wanted to ask you something."

"Okay."

Sebastian shifted to his knees and reached into the picnic basket.

James's heart jumped into his throat as excited nerves swirled in his chest. He'd just figured out what this was.

"James." Sebastian pulled something small from the basket, holding it hidden in his fist. "These past two years have been better than anything I've ever dreamed of. I love sharing my life with you, growing with you, and figuring out all my messy shit with you. You've always been there for me, and I feel so understood by you. I love you and want to spend the rest of my life with you."

Tears slid down James's cheeks. "I want to spend the rest of my life with you too, Sebastian."

He opened his hand to reveal a small black box, hazel eyes shining as they bore into James. "So you'll marry me then?"

"Yes, sweetheart. Yes, I'll marry you."

Sebastian flung himself on James, who caught him and buried his face in Sebastian's curls.

"You're trembling, sweetheart."

Sebastian laughed, repositioning himself so he straddled James's lap. "I don't know why that was so scary. It's not like I thought you'd turn me down."

"It's still nerve-wracking. I've been worrying about how to pop the question for months."

Sebastian's smile twisted slyly. "You have?"

"There's a ring for you in my sock drawer." James's cheeks strained from smiling. "I was going to take you away for the weekend and ask you then, but I like this better. Fuck, I love you so much."

Sebastian crashed their mouths together and kissed James fervently. James buried his hands in Sebastian's hair, happiness all but bursting out of him.

They broke apart, and Sebastian opened the little black box, revealing a thick, brushed silver band. "I got it engraved." He slipped it from the box and tilted it for James to see the underside.

Mine was etched in Sebastian's beautiful cursive.

James let out a happy whining sound. "It's perfect."

Sebastian slipped the ring on James's finger and pulled him into another drawn-out kiss.

"I can't wait to marry you," Sebastian said when they broke apart. "We'll be Mr. and Mr. Gray-Storm. It's the coolest last name I've ever heard."

"Ah, so the real reason you want me finally comes to light," James teased.

"Damn right. Your bedroom skills and name are all I want from you."

"Nightmare." James laughed as he kissed the shit-eating grin off Sebastian's face.

"But I'm your nightmare," Sebastian crooned. "You love me like this."

"I do." James cupped Sebastian's smiling face. "You're mine, and I love you exactly as you are."

"I'm yours," Sebastian agreed. "Forever."

The End

LOOKING for a bit more James and Sebastian? Don't miss *Making Plans* and other bonus scenes exclusive to my newsletter subscribers. Join now and see what James and Sebastian are planning for their wedding day!

HAVE you read Eli and Parker's story? *The Fall of Elijah Gray* is a stand-alone prequel novella to the Moonlight Falls trilogy, available now.

WANT TO KEEP IN TOUCH? Join my reader group on Facebook, Colette Rivera's Coven.

THANK YOU FOR READING THE
HEART OF MOONLIGHT FALLS

I hoped you enjoyed the final installment of James and Sebastian's story.

Reviews are invaluable to authors. Please consider leaving a review for *The Heart of Moonlight Falls* on your favorite review site or the site where you purchased this book to help others find magical books they'll love.

ACKNOWLEDGMENTS

Wow, we've made it to the end of Moonlight Falls! Thank you, Abbie Nicole, for working on this series with me. Your comments and editing really helped make these books the best they could be.

Thank you to Sleepy Fox Studio for the gorgeous cover design. I love seeing James and Sebastian together at last.

As always, thank you to TK for your love and support. I could not build these magic worlds without you.

And thank you to all my readers. I'm beyond thrilled how many people have fallen in love with Moonlight Falls. We're all Moonlighters at heart.

ABOUT THE AUTHOR

Colette is an author of queer paranormal romance novels. She loves to write couples who take care of each other and show their soft sides when in love. Sugar and spice are key ingredients in all her books. She's an avid PNR reader and loves all things magic. Colette once lived in the US but now calls New Zealand home. As a bisexual she has to resist making all her characters bi. When she succeeds you'll find a variety of representation in her books.

Colette can be found on Instagram @colette_rivera and on Facebook under Colette Rivera Author. She can also be found on her website coletterivera.com where you can sign up to her newsletter for bonus scenes and updates.

MOONLIGHT FALLS

The Fall of Elijah Gray

The Seduction of James Gray

The Cursed Sebastian Storm

The Heart of Moonlight Falls